For Maureen,

With warmest regards

Jack Harte

Airfield

14 April 2005

FROM UNDER GOGOL'S NOSE

JACK HARTE

For
John F Deane and Padraig J Daly

Author's Acknowledgements

Sincere thanks to Pat Pidgeon, Colm McHugh, Vergil Nemchev and all at Scotus. Also thanks to Henry Sharpe for permission to use the cover portrait and to Denis Bannister and Pat Pidgeon for their drawings. Special thanks to Tom Turley and Glendale Press who published 'Murphy in the Underworld', and John F Deane and Dedalus Press who published 'Birds and other Tails'.

Published in Ireland by
Scotus Press
PO Box 9498
Dublin 6

Copyright Jack Harte 1986, 1992, 1996, 2004

The moral right of the author has been asserted.

A catalogue record of this book is available from the British Library.
ISBN 0 9547194 0 9

All rights reserved. No part of this publication may be reproduced or transmitted in any form or by any means, electronic or mechanical, including photography, recording, or any information storage or retrieval system, without permission in writing from the publisher. The book is sold subject to the condition that it shall not, by way of trade or otherwise, be lent, resold or otherwise circulated without the publisher's prior consent in any form of binding or cover other than that in which it is published and without a similar condition, including this condition, being imposed on the subsequent purchaser.

Cover portrait of Jack Harte by Henry Sharpe.
Drawings on pages 56 and 120 by Denis Bannister
Drawings on pages 194 and 206 by Pat Pidgeon
Design and layout Pat Pidgeon and Colm McHugh

Contents

PREFACE

The State of the Irish Short Story   15
The Storyman Interview   31
The Great Silence   45

MURPHY IN THE UNDERWORLD

Murphy in the Underworld   57
Come, Follow Me   66
In the Retirement Colony   74
The Bleeding Stone of Knockaculleen   82
Baptism of Water   90
Gelding   95
Queen B   100
Three for Oblivion   107

BIRDS

A Message to Sparta   121
Painter   131
Bonds   136
Bike   144
Requiem for Johnny Murtagh   156
Turfman   166
Behind the Castle Walls   168
And What is the Thunder?   176
Distraction   181
O'Dowd and the Mermaid   184
Birds   193

PREFACE

THE STATE OF THE IRISH SHORT STORY

PART ONE

Irish Short Story
Irish Short Story
Irish Short Story
Irish Short Story
I S S
I S S

The happy happy tale of Little Iss and his Great Nanny

ISS NEVER KNEW FOR SURE HOW OR WHEN HE had come into the care of his nanny, who by reason of age was really his great nanny. It was one of those arrangements that seemed to exist without commencement or termination. There were the whispered rumours, of course, the wild speculations, the snide hints. But Great Nanny was emphatic in his declaration that he did not breed, beget, nor deliver the child. And so the enduring legend was that Iss had been deposited on the doorstep, all tucked up in a little basket like Moses in the bulrushes. There was a note which read: 'Take good care of him. His name is Isis. He is the gift of the gods'.

Little Iss had a lot to be grateful for. His great nanny was a most considerate and conscientious person, who decided on the spot to dedicate his whole life to the nurturing of this little foundling. And, yes, strange as it may seem, Great Nanny was a man.

Great Nanny's enthusiasm for rearing Little Iss was the marvel of the very fine neighbourhood in which they lived. No parent could have done more for him. No parent had a clearer or more defined vision of the man he wanted to fashion from this boy. No parent set about moulding the adult from the child with such unrelenting determination as did Great Nanny.

The first thing he tackled was the child's name, Isis. It was silly, declared Great Nanny, inappropriate, unacceptable. Besides, it stirred credence in the rumours of the boy's divine associations. 'Balderdash', was what Great Nanny called these superstitious mumblings, 'absolute balderdash'. The boy was merely the product of an accidental and unwanted pregnancy. 'It couldn't be simpler', Great Nanny declared, 'couldn't be more explicable, couldn't be more ordinary'.

And so he set to and excised the small 'i' from the boy's name, changing 'Isis' to 'Iss'. 'Too many eyes lead to confusion,' he joked to himself as he sat back and admired his work.

Although Iss mourned the loss of his small 'i', that seemingly inoffensive little stick with the knob on top, he nevertheless rejoiced in his cool masculine tag, and basked in the satisfaction that the operation had given his great nanny.

Iss grew up in Great Nanny's large comfortable house and its spacious meticulously cultivated garden. Such was the solicitude of his guardian that Iss was never absent from his watchful gaze, even for the space of a minute, during his infant years. And when he came of school-going age, Great Nanny would not entrust his education to the teachers in the local school. Instead, he converted one of the rooms into a classroom and set about teaching Little Iss everything he needed to know.

This happy happy domestic relationship continued through the boy's childhood and into adolescence. Eventually, needless to say, Iss began to express a wish to explore the neighbourhood, to make friends, to meet people. But Great Nanny, ever anxious, would have none of it. Instead, Great Nanny selected a few suitable friends who were invited over to play with Iss in the garden or to engage in conversation with him in the plush sitting room. But they were never inclined to return. 'Boring', they said. 'Nothing to do', they said. The criticism was totally unfair, Great Nanny convinced himself. The garden had tightly cropped lawns and little figurines as ornaments strewn around strategically. What more could little boys want?

And so Iss was left to wander alone through the spacious house, or to sprawl for hours in the deck chair staring at the sky.

Eventually his frustration, his boredom, his loneliness, got the better of him. Eventually his curiosity led him to wonder what kind of world lay beyond the back wall of the garden. It faced south and Iss imagined a sunlit place where brightly clad people with tanned faces gathered in throngs to sell and buy exotic trinkets in crowded bazaars. Silly, but that was what the youth imagined lay just beyond that rampart at the end of the garden.

There was a heavy wooden door in the back wall and this door and the world behind it grew into an obsession with him. So one day when there was no sign of Great Nanny in the garden, he pulled over the tool bunker and reached up to slam back the heavy bolt. He replaced the bunker. Then, breathless with expectancy, he opened the door.

Outside, with his arms folded, a satisfied grin on his big round face, was Great Nanny. It was as if he had been there all along just waiting for Iss to attempt this sortie.

"Please, Great Nanny," the youth pleaded, "I have heard that there are sunlit landscapes to the south and I would dearly love to see them, just once."

"Nonsense," replied Great Nanny, coming in and bolting the door. "If you want to admire the magic of a sunlit landscape, go and watch the rose-bed at noon. Believe me, there is nothing more wonderful than that outside the walls of this garden."

Iss tried most assiduously to interest himself in the roses, for he was always anxious to please Great Nanny. After all, Great Nanny had been so good to him. However, he soon found his imagination wandering again and his eye squinting through the chinks of the door in the east wall, especially in the morning as the sun was rising. When he could resist his curiosity no longer he pulled a garden chair over to the door and slid the bolt back gently. But when he opened the door, lo and behold, who was outside with his beaming face and wagging finger, only Great Nanny!

"Please, Great Nanny, I have watched the crimson streaks in the morning sky, and I would love to see the sun just as it rises above the horizon," said Iss, "just once, please."

"You'll see it soon enough," replied Great Nanny, bolting the door emphatically, "when it shines across the garden wall, and it will be all the more realistic for being well used by the world at mid-morning."

It was a while before Iss felt the urge to explore again. But sprawled in the deck-chair he watched the cloud formations in the evening illuminated by the setting sun. And he noticed that when the twilight was thickening there was a trail of dark birds across the sky, rooks probably, beating their heavy way towards the west. And he wondered where they roosted and why they returned so faithfully night after night from their foraging expeditions.

One evening when the sky was filled with puffy clouds and the procession of dark birds towards the west seemed endless, poor Iss could no longer restrain himself. He crept down to the door in the west wall and used the garden hoe to slide back the heavy bolt. He opened the door cautiously, and somehow was not surprised but was certainly disappointed to find a stern-faced Great Nanny looking at him with a hurt expression on his face.

"Forgive me," said Iss resignedly. "I was curious to see what dark wood was so attractive as to lure back the wandering rooks from their daily travels."

"What nonsense," replied Great Nanny, slamming the door closed to indicate his annoyance, "when you can admire the finches and the linnets that come to feed from the bird-table in the garden every day."

Iss was wracked with guilt. He was so contrite for having offended Great Nanny that he never attempted another sortie from that day on. Indeed he banished every thought of the world outside the garden walls. He grew into a very cultivated young man, whom his neighbours admired enormously, even if their offspring dismissed him as effete and colourless. Above all, his neighbours admired the assiduousness with which he dedicated himself to his Great Nanny. Yes, he took it upon himself to wait on Great Nanny, hand and foot, and to atone for his youthful disloyal thoughts and urges by answering every call, serving every whim of his dear dear Great Nanny. Thus he felt he was slowly making restitution to Great Nanny who had been so good to him.

Eventually no one bothered to visit anymore. Old neighbours died, and the new young neighbours who took their places showed scant interest in the two men who were growing old together - for, old as Great Nanny was, it seemed that Iss was rapidly catching up on him. And the two ageing men did not bother their neighbours either, but kept to themselves, keeping their house tidy, their garden trim, and showing the utmost courtesy and consideration to one another, for they continued to admire each other absolutely. Yes, Great Nanny was as proud and protective of his charge as ever, with Iss, now almost as feeble as his Great Nanny, still labouring away to repay his immense debt of gratitude. And whenever the new young neighbours caught a glimpse of the two men, or encountered them on their way to the shop, they could never quite tell which was Iss and which was Great Nanny.

Part Two

Iss – What now?

ONE MORNING ISS ROSE FROM HIS BED, drawing himself out of the weight of his sleep. He stepped carefully into the bathroom and closed the door. To his surprise he saw the reflection of Great Nanny in the mirror, and blurted out an apology and a greeting. But the sounds echoed against the walls of the hollow cell. There was no one there but himself.

Iss stood rooted in the centre of the bathroom. He was totally awake now, and shocked. He looked again into the big mirror. It was his own reflection that had played the trick on him. He examined this image. Truly the resemblance was remarkable. In every line and feature, in set and expression, the image in the mirror was as faithful a reflection of Great Nanny as it was of him.

He went back to bed and lay thinking for a long time. He had been conscious of how assiduously he had sought to please Great Nanny in every way, to obey every admonition, to comply with every preference. But now it seemed to oppress him that he had succeeded so well there was not a single trace of his own individual personality left.

Had he ever been individual, different? He could not recall. Yet deep down he had a sense that he could have been different, should have been different, a sense of myriad lost opportunities, away back. Would it have been such treason if he had followed some of those urges, explored some of those possibilities?

In spite of lying in bed most of the day pondering these

thoughts, Iss did not feel closer to a resolution of any of them. He eventually put on his clothes and went into the living room where Great Nanny was still reading the morning papers as was his custom.

"Have you been out of sorts?" asked Great Nanny, without looking up from the newspaper.

"Yes," replied Iss. "I have been wondering what I would have discovered had I been allowed to go out the garden gates when I was a boy. Remember how you stopped me each time."

Great Nanny lowered the paper, a look of amazement, incredulity, on his face. "Surely you are not referring to those times when you were a boy and had silly ideas as to the world outside."

"I am indeed," said Iss. "And I now regret that I was not more adventurous. Do you know that I have become so like you that people on the street cannot tell us apart? Would you believe that when I looked in the mirror this morning, I thought for a moment it was you I was looking at."

"Is that such a bad thing?" asked Great Nanny with a look of smug satisfaction on his face.

Iss stared at him. It was absolutely clear to him that Great Nanny could never understand his predicament and that it was useless to take the conversation further. He took a big deep breath.

"I have decided to go now and look for all those things I felt so close to finding when I was a boy."

"Don't be ridiculous. At your age! Surely you realise at this stage that everything out there in the world is perfectly ordinary."

"Maybe so, but there might still be something wonderful to be experienced. So I must go now, before it is too late."

"Go if you must," replied Great Nanny in a peeved and sulky voice. "But if you go, the door closes behind you, and you do not come back. I certainly can't have you around this house with your head full of woolly ideas, ready to act on any whim that seizes you."

"So be it," said Iss. And without packing a bag, without saying goodbye, he got up, walked out into the garden and looked about. Above him the trail of rooks across the sky pointed towards the setting sun. It was a sign, sign enough, reminder enough, for Iss. He went to the door in the west wall of the garden, opened it decisively and walked through. He didn't bother to close it behind him.

He followed the flight of the dark birds and very soon he discovered their destination, a large park, full of leafy trees, surrounded by a high green railing. Iss skirted the railing until he came to a large gate. People were streaming out and someone was tolling a hand-bell inside as if driving these people before him. Obviously, the warden was about to close the park for the night. Iss slipped inside the gate and veered off behind some trees into a shrubbery. There he crouched to the ground, hidden from the searching eyes of the warden and the world.

In a short while silence reigned, silence but for the grumbling of the rooks as they settled in their roost above his head. Iss sat against the base of the tree, looking up at the rooks, at the darkening sky above them. He felt alone and terrified, but mixed through the terror and the loneliness was another feeling, a sort of counter-feeling that his terror and his loneliness were natural and right. And he felt little twinges of satisfaction too, satisfaction that he had finally taken a step all on his own, a step away from Great Nanny, a step towards reclaiming his own individual personality, or perhaps establishing it, as it hardly ever existed.

When the quiet had finally settled on the park, Iss began to think of the implications of his action. He had no shelter, nowhere to sleep, nothing to eat. And yet he was not daunted by these consequences.

He arose and began to move slowly around the park, admiring the trees and the pond, and the slumbering ducks as if he were seeing such things for the very first time.

Iss was relieved to see right in the middle of the park a large covered bandstand. At least he would have somewhere to shelter from the elements. As he approached the bandstand he noticed dark figures moving furtively in the same direction. He was not alone in the park. About half a dozen men gathered under the bandstand, muttering greetings of familiarity to one another. They all looked curiously at Iss, but only in the way people examine someone new to the group, not challenging his right to be there. Some had blankets or covering of one kind or another and were curling up on the ground. Others took out cigarettes and bottles and huddled in a group on a bench that ran along the back of the stand. Iss sat adjacent to this huddle.

Eventually one of the men offered him a swig from his bottle, but Iss declined.

"What has you here, then?" asked the man.

"I'm not sure," replied Iss. "Trying to find myself."

The man chuckled. "You'll have a hard job finding yourself here, unless you've brought yourself along."

"I don't know who I am. I don't know where I came from. I don't know what I'm supposed to be doing."

"You're in a bad way alright."

"And I don't know who to ask for help."

"You should try Mr O'Connor."

"Who is he?" asked Iss.

"Mr O'Connor. He's the wisest man I know. Comes to the park every day and sits on the bench over there looking up at the sky. Gave me the price of this bottle today, he did. There he was with this young fellow flitting around him. 'Look at that cloud,' said the young fellow. 'Doesn't it look like a bit of wool tossed up into the sky?' With that I nipped up to Mr O'Connor. 'Could you give me a few coppers to buy a drink?' Mr O'Connor burst out laughing and clapped his hands on his knees. 'There you are,' he said to the young fellow. 'That's a lesson in directness for you. No blather about wool tossed into the sky there.' He turned out his pockets and gave me every last penny he had in change. Yes, Mr O'Connor is the man to consult."

That night Iss tried with difficulty to sleep sitting upright on the bench, reluctant to stretch out on the ground like the others.

The next day he waited around the bandstand, watching the seat that Mr O'Connor was wont to occupy. He was dubious of success, but had decided to try every possibility in future.

Eventually a portly gentleman with a thin moustache came along and sat in that very seat. Iss knew from his bearing and

his demeanour that this must be Mr O'Connor.
He went over and sat on the other end of the park bench.
"Would you be Mr O'Connor?" he ventured to ask.
"I might be. Can I help you?"
"I'm trying to find out who I am, where I came from," replied Iss.

Mr O'Connor turned and examined Iss with a benevolent, sympathetic gaze. After a few moments he said, "Read Gogol. We all came out from under Gogol's Overcoat."

His pronouncement had a ring of authority about it, and a note of finality.

Without further ado Iss thanked Mr O'Connor and took his leave of him. He made his way out of the park and along the high street until he found the Public Library.

The assistant was able to locate a volume of Gogol very quickly, and Iss spent the day reading the volume.

He read 'The Overcoat' and many of the other works in the volume, but found no answer to his question. In fact he came up with a new question to put to Mr O'Connor: 'If we all came out from under Gogol's 'Overcoat', then who came out from under Gogol's 'Nose'?'

He returned to slip into the park before the bellman closed the gate.

That night tiredness laid him flat among the stretched figures on the floor of the bandstand.

When he awoke the next morning his shoes were gone, taken clean off his feet and a pair of battered torn runners left beside him. The last of the men were leaving, melting into the undergrowth before the bellman commenced his opening round, but they just shrugged in response to his protestation.

He had no choice but to put on the runners. They added very much to the effect of his crumpled clothes, his growing stubble: he was rapidly becoming one with the inhabitants of the bandstand, rapidly becoming a tramp. He was getting hungry too, very hungry; soon he would have to beg for food or for the coppers to buy it. And yet Iss was not ashamed of this condition; on the contrary he felt a surge of pride, a self-respect that he had never felt before.

He waited in the park that day keeping Mr O'Connor's seat under observation. The question burned within him like a piece of hot metal, and he wanted to put the question to Mr O'Connor. He felt no closer to discovering where he had come from, and wanted to know why he felt he might have come from under Gogol's 'Nose' rather than Gogol's 'Overcoat' as Mr O'Connor had suggested. He also thought he might touch the man for the price of a sandwich.

But Mr O'Connor didn't appear that day, or the next day either. And when Iss enquired of one of the gentlemanly regulars he was told, 'Poor Mr O'Connor won't be back anymore'. That was all, but Iss knew the rest.

He was distraught. Mr O'Connor had left him with a question rather than an answer. And now he didn't know where to turn. He went out and stood for a while at the gate of the park, begging, but people veered clear of him, and it took him several hours to collect the price of a sandwich. Then he was turned away from two shops as he tried to enter. The third shop was busy and he had picked up the sandwich and handed the money to the check-out girl before anyone could stop him.

That night he began to feel wretched. After he had eaten his sandwich he curled up for the night into a little knot of misery. To make matters worse, he thought he heard one of the men snigger to another, 'Look at him now. He doesn't much look like the gift of the gods, does he?'

Part Three

Iss – Back to where it all began?

Iss slept soundly enough, perhaps as a result of the accumulated tiredness, perhaps because of the comfort of the food inside him. The park was open when he awoke, and people were coming and going. To his surprise he saw a girl, a young woman, sitting on the bench of the bandstand quite close to him. All the other men had gone.

He began to pull himself together and to smooth down his clothes.

"Will you look at the state of you!" said the girl.

Iss was taken aback, first at the fact that the girl had spoken to him instead of hurrying away, then at the impudence of the remark.

"I beg your pardon," he blurted. "What business is it of yours how I look?"

"If it's not my business, then it's nobody's business."

"Who might you be then?" he asked with sarcasm.

"Your mother."

Iss guffawed, genuinely amused. "If you said you were my daughter, there might be a basis for credibility, except that I have never participated in the act of generation."

"No, you haven't been very productive, have you? And you are old and haggard enough to be my father, but that's all of your own doing."

"If you were my mother you would have no right to berate me, believe me."

"I am your mother, and I have every right. Didn't I leave you with that Great Nanny of yours who had such a puffed-up reputation? Didn't I expect he would give you the perfect rearing?

Alright, I was wrong, he turned out to be a dry old stick, but that was no reason for you turning yourself into a dry old stick as well in order to be like him."

"You left me and ran." Iss surprised himself by his own acceptance that this very lovely young woman was in fact his mother.

"I had other things to do."

"And you left a silly note, giving me a girl's name."

"It was not a silly note. It was sincere. And the name I gave you was a fine one, an appropriate one, the name of a god."

"A female god."

"One of the greatest of the gods. What if she was a woman? All men should be given women's names, to remind them that they're more female than they think. And look what you let them do to you. Pluck out one of your eyes, to make you more masculine! What nonsense. You let them remove the depth from your vision, in order to disguise your true nature. You have ended up a sorry mess, you have."

"I won't dispute that," replied Iss resignedly. "But what can I do about it now? One eye I have lost. One eye I have left."

"Get rid of it."

"The other eye?"

"Yes, get rid of it."

"Then how shall I see?"

"You haven't seen very well with it. You see a world that is flat, a shallow world that bears no relationship to the truth. Yes, your single eye leaves you with an impoverished vision. Better to get rid of it, and see instead with your imagination. Here."

And she came towards him, leaned over him, and plucked out painlessly his remaining eye. His final sight was of that beautiful young woman, her hair falling about her face, her breasts reaching towards him. Then that gentle tweak, and all was darkness.

He was silent for a while as he strained to see with the empty sockets.

"Now I can no longer call myself Iss. Now I must be Ss."

"Whatever."

"But that's not a name I like. It sounds as if the bearer is asleep: Ss."

"So what?"

"Or that I'm admonishing all to silence: Ss."

"That might not be so misplaced, considering they have so little to say, most of them. Why not cut the duplication then and simply call yourself S?"

"Yes, S, that sounds crisp and emphatic, don't you think? And what shall I call you? You never said your name."

"I'm not as hung up on names as you appear to be. Names are of dubious usefulness, often hiding the truth instead of pointing towards it."

"But I must have some name for you. How else can I refer even to this conversation? I can hardly say, 'She said this, and she did that'."

"Why not?"

"Alright then, I shall call you She."

"That's alright with me, if it's alright with you."

They settled then into an easy silence, S trying to recall what She looked like, and the more he recalled her features the more beautiful she became. Eventually he broke the silence.

"What was all that nonsense, in your note, about my being the gift of the gods?"

"It was no nonsense. That's what you were, the gift of the gods." She laughed. "And look at the state of you now."

"I don't understand," said S. "I don't understand anything."

"You will. As soon as you start seeing with your imagination. How can you understand, when you have learned to use so few of your faculties? Even the pitiful few you did learn to use, you have turned into handicaps. However, it's never too late. You can still learn to understand, to recognise the truth without looking for its ID. To recognise it by the faintest sensation in your toes, or by the sudden explosion in the front of your brain."

"Will you be around to teach me these things?"

She gave an amused chuckle. "I will and I won't. You know me - I'll be everywhere and anywhere. I'll be there if you really want to find me. Just don't expect me to come running if you start moping in self-pity. I can't stand that."

"At least stay until you have told me everything about myself."

"There you go again. What do you want from me? Your CV? Your Birth Certificate? It's up to you to create your own CV; the only CV that's important is the one for the future and that has yet to be written. And as for a birth certificate, you have been born a thousand times, which one do you want certified?"

After this little outburst She was silent for a while, and S was overwhelmed, trying to make sense of what she was saying.

"It's frustrating the way people want everything spelt out. I could just as easily have put it the other way around, you know, that the gods were your gift to the world. Would they have made more sense of that? And of course it's true. Yes, it's going back a long way. A long long way. But that's as far back as you go. You are of an age with the gods." She was chuckling again. "And you look it."

But S was too overawed to be amused by her joke. He was terrified too. He knew, perhaps by the sensation in his toes, that She was not going to stay much longer, and he wanted some useful advice lest his new predicament be ten times worse than his old.

"What do you advise me to do now?" he asked in as matter-of-fact a tone as he could manage, lest she think he was returning to wallowing in self-pity and leave him on the spot.

"You've learned how to beg, why not turn to busking? Why not sing for your supper, as they say?"

"I can't sing. I don't know any songs. And without a single eye I can't even make it to the gate of the park."

"No, but you can learn to sing, if you open your ears and open your mouth. You can feel your way to the gate of the park, if you put your hands out in front of you. And as for songs, the best ones have yet to be composed, so why not make up your own?"

S thought about this for a while and slowly worked out the implications, how he could manage to get to the park gate, and the shop, and back to the bandstand. Reasonably satisfied with the plan of action, he replied: "Okay, I'll do it."

But his words travelled on through an empty silence, and he knew She was no longer there.

S became a feature just outside the main gate of the park, the blind beggar who chanted in a voice that no one had ever heard before, who sang songs that were unlike anything people had ever heard before. The very few people who paused to listen out of curiosity, and lingered out of interest, threw coins in his upturned cap, and came back again and again, wondering.

Every day S tried to see a little more by the brightening dawn of his imagination, and he tried to fashion songs that were joyful and tragic out of the experience of his thousand births and his thousand deaths. And he tried to dredge songs too out of the accumulated loneliness of his thousand lives, from that time long ago when a man first stood on a mountaintop and looked with terror and with wonder at the confusion of stars in the night sky, before returning full of speculation to his wide-eyed people, to explain the fire in the spears of lightning and the anger in the thunder's roll. And all the while he was singing, S was also hoping that people out there were listening, hoping that one day they would know what he was offering them - the gift of the gods.

THE STORYMAN INTERVIEW

I *TRACED HIM TO A FLAT IN A SOUTH DUBLIN suburb where he had been living in isolation and obscurity for several decades. His so-called flat was no more than an old-style bed-sitter, nowadays glorified by estate agents with the name, 'studio apartment'. The clutter of books and tea-cups, sheets of paper scribbled on and discarded, packets of sliced bread half-consumed, an open carton of rancid-looking butter, all attested to continuing intellectual activity in the midst of domestic squalor.*

When he heard the purpose of my visit, that I was pursuing a course in creative writing and wished to make him the subject of my dissertation, he guffawed. He laughed with genuine mirth, then, it seemed to me, laughed with pity. He prepared two cups of coffee, handed one to me, pushed an opened packet of chocolate goldgrain biscuits in my direction, and sat back. I cleared a corner of the table and set up my tape recorder, the microphone pointing towards him, arranged my note pad with the carefully composed questions on my knee, and sat back too, waiting for him to talk.

- So where do we start?

- At the beginning, I suppose.

- In the beginning ..... was the Word. And Word begat Story, and Story begat God and all of the heavenly hosts. How's that? ..... When I was a young man ..... I fell in love ..... with the short story. Is that better?

Yes, and Story begat Moses and Jesus and Mohammed. And Story begat Lugh of the Long Rays, and Cuchulainn, and Fionn.....

When Yeats was an old man ..... someone asked him, as someone would, to whom did he see the mantle of Irish literature passing after he had departed. Yeats is said to have replied, 'the Cork Realists'.

Hard to believe!

The Cork Realists. Daniel Corkery, and Sean O'Faolain, and Frank O'Connor, and Elizabeth Bowen. And Liam O'Flaherty who wasn't a Corkman at all.

Hard to believe that in the nineteen thirties people read short stories and cherished short story writers.

Hard to believe that in 1963 Frank O'Connor published 'The Lonely Voice' and claimed that the short story was Ireland's national art form. And no one contradicted him.

Hard to believe that in 2003, the centenary of his birth, O'Connor is almost forgotten, and his beloved short story eclipsed almost to the point of extinction.

And the wise men can't understand it. It goes against reason, they say. The short story is the literary genre that most aptly conveys the fragmentary nature of modern life and modern experience. That's what they say. So why is there no interest in it? The hurly-burly of contemporary living allows only snatches of time for reading. So why do people not avail of such intermissions to read short stories? That's what the wise men ask. Why do publishers want whoppers of novels instead of collections of crafted short stories? Why do newspapers and magazines no longer print individual stories? Why? Why?

So many whys from the wise men on this subject, so few answers.

He paused, and once more lapsed back into the chair for a few moments in silence. Then he sprang forward again, his elbows planted on his knees.

- If we are going to search for an answer, we must begin with one simple honest truth: there is no longer any significant public for the short story. People do not read short stories. They are not interested.

If there were avid readers waiting for short stories then newspapers and magazines would be carrying them. If there was a demand for collections of stories by specialist story writers, then they would be welcomed by the publishers. The reality is that a collection of stories is as welcome in a publishing house as a pork chop in a synagogue. The reality is that when a magazine or newspaper carries a short story, it is either out of a sense of noble obligation, or out of nostalgia for the glorious past of the genre. The reality is that there is no public demand for the short story. And that is the reality we must start from.

- *But there are some masters of the story, still alive, still writing stories, McGahern, William Trevor, Benedict Kiely.*

- True, but three swallows don't make a summer. And some writers from the younger generations have written good stories too, but that doesn't alter the climate either. Take the three you mentioned. In each case their stories are superior to their novels, but while their novels are read widely from generation to generation, their stories are barely kept in print. And if they had never written a novel, would their stories have carried them to the same pinnacle of literary esteem? I think not. And as soon as a young writer, like yourself, issues a good story he is immediately advised to channel his efforts into a novel. Agents, publishers, editors, commentators, all join the conspiracy to siphon off new talent from the short story. And if that promising writer persists with the short story, he is advised at least to write a novel as well so that he will gain a readership. The logic there is that no one will be interested in reading stories for their own sake, and can be persuaded to read them only out of interest in the author as a novelist or as a celebrity.

- *If the situation is that bad, then it can only get better.*

- No, it can get worse. Writers can lose interest in it. In spite of the dreadful state of the short story from the point of view of publication and readership, it still has a powerful appeal for writers. And it's easy to understand why. The writing of the most banal short story challenges the skill and the invention of a writer to an extent that the writing of a novel can never do. The satisfaction of having forged a short story out of unyielding conditions is the only satisfaction left the writer, but it is still enough to encourage the effort. But perhaps you are right. Perhaps that is the bedrock, the level below which we are unlikely to sink. If so, we should use it as a foundation. Certainly lamenting its decline will do nothing to improve the state of the short story. But neither will the deluding cant that accompanies the publication of the occasional anthology, that the short story is still alive, still thriving, still being fostered in Cork.

- *To what do you attribute the decline of the short story?*

- Whom do we blame? That's a good question. If we could find the culprit and eliminate him, all would be well. If we could find the cause and tackle it, then we might start making progress again. Do we attribute the decline to the disappearance of the traditional outlets in magazines and newspapers? No, that would not be logical, would it? That would be to mistake the effect for the cause, the symptom for the disease. Do we blame the dull editorial policy that has pervaded for the last forty years, that has canonised Cork Realism and reduced it from a diamond to a lump of domestic coal? Perhaps. Yes, that certainly accelerated the decline. That is closer to the prime cause. Add to that the reduction of the short story to a practice range for aspiring novelists, and you get the realist approach drilled in. What is being placed uppermost in the mind of the young writer is to show from the story he is writing that he has the capability of being a novelist, and to write in a manner that will convince a particular editor or agent of that capability. The production line of these made-to-measure stories is endless and the tedium for the reader close to absolute. Then the claims that are made that this is good for the short story! It drives me to distraction. The form has traditionally suffered from being cast in a secondary role to the novel, but today it has been downgraded further in the hierarchy of esteem, downgraded to the status of a shoeshine.

The Storyman Interview

- *So you blame editorial policy for the short story's decline?*

- This straitjacket of Cork Realism has certainly been a major factor. Every damn story has to be a slice-of-life. Every story has to explore a significant moment, a moment of crisis, a turning point in the life of the subject. Every story has to strain for an epiphany in the most mundane situations. And the stories are so predictable in their banality that there is no longer the remotest chance of surprise for the reader. Fine, if some stories want to do that, but there is a life elsewhere, and there is a story elsewhere. Cork Realism may have been very good for the development of the novel, and that's for a different discussion. But we are concerned with the fate of the short story, and I believe one of the main reasons for the stunting of its growth lies in the stultifying misunderstanding of the form, down through the generations, by critics, by commentators, by the reading public, a misunderstanding which has isolated it on this barren headland of Cork Realism.

- *Do you not think that O'Connor's 'Lonely Voice' provides an adequate insight into the form?*

- Have you read it?

- *Yes, it is the core text on our short story course.*

- Indeed. A core text on everybody's short story course, that's the trouble. It is everybody's anchor in the unexplored sea of the short story, everybody's point of departure and point of return. But I'll tell you this much, if the novel is an ocean liner and the short story a coaster, as people are fond of saying, then 'The Lonely Voice' is the lighthouse guiding them on their way, and it's no wonder the short story has run aground.

- *I would have presumed you liked Frank O'Connor.*

- I don't like Frank O'Connor. I love him. I worship him. Why do you think I live next door to where he wrote 'Guests of the Nation'? Have you never seen me late at night touching the latch on his old gate with reverence? His stories should be recited by the angels. But his book on the short story is full of balderdash. It should be taken with a grain of salt instead of being received as the bread of heaven.

- *That's severe, considering how influential the book has been.*

- But that's the problem, isn't it, that it has been so influential. If people read it as an insight into O'Connor's approach to story-writing, that would be fine, but to slavishly adopt it and adhere to it, as if every dictum came directly from the tablets of stone, shows gross stupidity. A moment's reflection on his peremptory generalisations should be enough for any intelligent reader to realise that in many of them he was wildly off target. Look at his explanation of the different conditions in which the short story and the novel thrive. Without the concept of a normal society the novel is impossible, he says, and normal society he envisages as the structured stratified society that existed in England up to his day. Since the sixties considerable disintegration of this normal society has taken place in England and the ranks of submerged population groups have swollen and have become very articulate, conditions ideal for the nurture of the short story, it would seem, yet it is the novel that continues to thrive and in England too the short story is facing extinction. In Ireland even the social and family structures that existed in O'Connor's day have been fragmented, have disintegrated almost, a condition which should have been favourable to the continued thriving of the short story, inimical to the development of the novel. And look what happened – the exact opposite.

- *Are you blaming O'Connor himself, or his readers and followers?*

- Oh, I blame O'Connor too. He narrowed down the short story to his type of short story, the study of the critical moment, the crucial event. And he was intolerant of any variation. He quoted Turgenev, and agreed with him, that 'we all came out from under Gogol's "Overcoat".' But, even as he is agreeing, you can sense the itch in his fingers to take up the pen and re-write the story eliminating the ghost at the end. He was totally focused, and that is good for the writer, but it is the same as being blinkered, and that is bad for the critic or commentator or editor. If we all came out from under Gogol's "Overcoat", then who came out from under Gogol's "Nose"? Plenty, dearly beloved Frank, plenty, but you had ways of rationalising them out of bounds.

- *What about his thesis that the short story is essentially the voice of human loneliness?*

- More balderdash. He got that idea from his mentor, Corkery, who claimed much the same for music. Corkery suggested that the breath of life that is behind all great music is the sigh of loneliness. So do we go through all the arts and find that loneliness is the motivating factor in them all? I don't think so. Loneliness is one common aspect of human experience, as natural as pain, as pleasure, as love. Just as pain is an in-built protective mechanism to ensure the welfare of the body, so the capacity for loneliness is a natural protective mechanism to ensure the cohesion of the tribe. So why should the short story be limited to exploring loneliness when it can just as well explore love, pleasure, pain? And as for his submerged populations, his motley crew of outsiders, his tramps, artists, lonely idealists, dreamers, and spoiled priests, it is ludicrous to assume that they must be present in society in order to be re-created in the short story, since they are merely convenient figures on whom is projected the loneliness that is the natural experience of everyone. Cork Realism and the psychological study of outsiders may be cosy bed-fellows, but they beget only one kind of story.

- *Is it O'Connor's definition of the short story that you take issue with?*

- It is his whole obsession with definition, with limitation. And when he arrives at the formula for the short story as he sees it –the Cork Realist formula – he sets it down as canon, and any story that does not conform to that canon is other-than-a-short-story. It is a conte, or a nouvelle, or a tale. And to this day critics are snagged on the same spike, making up names such as metafiction, anti-stories, or fictions, for those stories that have been left off-side by the line O'Connor has drawn across the pitch. What a sterilising exercise it has all been! It is like arriving at a definition of the poem that covers only the lyric, and then holding that anything else is other-than-a-poem.

- So how would you define the short story?

- I wouldn't. Why bother? For the purpose of understanding the concept, the two words can't be made simpler. With basic concepts and objects you let experience do the job of definition. If you want a child to know what a hammer is, you hold up the tool and say, 'hammer'. Then experience impresses on the child its multiplicity of design and use. Whereas if you start with a definition, you sow the seed of confusion in the child's mind – if a man bludgeons another to death with a hammer, does it have to be re-defined to incorporate 'offensive weapon', or at that moment is it other-than-a-hammer? You might not see the relevance of this, but it is relevant, and the problem is central to the understanding and the use of the short story. Listen to this.

He went over to the bookshelves, rooted out a well-worn paperback copy of 'The Lonely Voice', and fingered through it.

- When O'Connor draws his line across the pitch with his narrow definition, he ends up with absurd conclusions. This is how he dismisses the later stories of DH Lawrence: 'The man was a flaming romantic anyhow, and I find myself reading those later stories in which he represents himself as a benevolent god, game-keeper, gypsy, stallion, or sunlight come on earth to relieve wealthy women of their sexual frustrations, as fairytales, legends, prose poems, anything on God's earth except a representation of human life and destiny'. Clearly Lawrence's stories did not fit the canon of Cork Realism. But listen to what he has to say about Mary Lavin, then a younger writer whom he greatly admired: 'With her growing power has come a certain irritable experimentation as in "The Widow's Son" where she experiments dangerously with alternative endings.' 'Experiments dangerously'! Wow! Frank was not one for throwing caution to the wind. There you have the negative spirit of Cork Realism that we have inherited. And listen to this for balderdash, again about Lavin: 'Her most important work will not be in the novel, nor in the short story form but in the nouvelle.' That's where you end up when you start off by defining and limiting. We should instead dedicate ourselves to freeing the short story of all limitation. A short story is a short story. Let's see what it can do. Let's see what we can do with it. Let it sprout wings and fly. Let it veer deliriously from one extreme to another. Let it skim so close to the discursive essay that it almost, but not quite, becomes one. Let it veer so close to the poem that it is preserved from absorption only by its narrative soul.

- But surely we must to some extent define the realm of the short story, for example to distinguish it from the novel.

- Yes, of course, the novel. That's part of the obsession, isn't it? The critics and the commentators regard the short story as the bastard son of the novel, whose status is dubious, and esteem low, whose existence and qualities have to be related to his supposed parent. But they are wrong. The short story is no bastard son of the novel. A better argument could be made for the reverse. But apart from that, the novel is the literary genre that the short story is most unlike. And the genre it is closest to is the poem, but no one seems to recognise that.

- The short story is closer to the poem than to the novel?

- Yes, and I'll tell you why. Firstly, both are fundamentally oral forms and work best when directed at the mind's ear. Secondly, the short story, like the poem, communicates primarily to the imagination, whereas the novel communicates primarily to the rational mind. That is why the short story is misunderstood, and why it does not enjoy mass popularity. It makes the reader work. As with the poem, the reader has to engage actively with the short story, has to participate in the creative process, has to activate his own narrative imagination. If the story does not demand this of the reader, or if the reader is too lazy to respond, then the special magic of the short story is lost.

Storytelling is as old as communication, even older than poetry. Indeed the very evolution of the mind seems to have been deeply and intimately and indelibly influenced by this faculty, this story faculty, this urge to create, hear, process stories. Anyway, storytelling has been around since people first spoke, and ever since they have been using story to explore and explain everything from the experience of their own lives to the mysteries of the universe. They have been using it to invent communal, tribal, religious identity. But always there has been the ever-present overriding urge to influence one another and entertain one another.

- But surely this storytelling tradition has been dissipated in modern times into all the narrative arts, the novel, drama, film, as well as the short story?

- Of course it has. But what is special about the short story is that it has remained closest to the ancient tradition of storytelling. It is the contemporary form that has evolved directly from the first primitive attempts at storytelling, down through myths and legends, folktales, fairytales, fables, the later literary tales, down to the magazine stories of the 19th Century. And the rest is well-recorded history. All other narrative forms are off-shoots, tangents, adaptations of narrative for different purposes. The short story is the pure and direct heir of the storytelling tradition because it essentially employs the same methods by communicating through the mind's ear directly to the imagination.

Because the printing of stories in magazines corresponded with the serialisation of and the growth of interest in novels, O'Connor, and indeed others, assumed that the two were related, that the short story had been invented from the spare rib of the novel. Nothing could be further from the truth. The rise of the magazines merely provided the story, which had been alive and thriving in the oral tradition, with the opportunity of evolving into a form more suited to the demands of the time.

- In what way are the methods of the short story closer to the

The Storyman Interview

storytelling tradition than, say, those of the novel?

- No doubt, on your course, you have studied the critics and are familiar with the common observations on the relative techniques of the two forms. They claim that the distinctive techniques of the short story have been developed to cope with the restraints of brevity. Whereas the novel has the space to be explicit in all things the short story is obliged to be implicit, to use suggestion as a technique for coping with the lack of space. And of course that is true. However, if you disregard this implication that the short story is struggling with the handicap of not being a novel, and look at it as a form in its own right, a form which communicates directly to the imagination, then the implicit, suggestive techniques are native to it, natural to it, and not adopted for ulterior reasons. The novel presents everything, explains everything, and the individual passive reader receives it pretty much as every other reader does, pretty much as the author conceived it. But the short story communicates in a totally different way. It is like a hand-grenade lobbed into the mind of the reader and when it makes contact with the active imagination of the reader it explodes, becomes something different, bigger, leaving the reader to trace the trajectories of the explosion.

- *That is what Poe talked about, is it not? The single powerful effect of the short story.*

- Yes and no. The impact of the grenade making contact is a single effect, the one Poe was speaking about, but the explosion and its aftermath are anything but single or simple. Perhaps if I use another, less violent, metaphor, I can better demonstrate the different phases in the communication of a short story. Think of the story as a stone, an object made from words, which the writer drops into the well of the mind. The immediate powerful impact comes when it hits the water and sets up a clear strong complete circular wave of meaning. However, the effect does not stop there. As the water settles there are further circular waves, not as powerful as the first perhaps but still complete. Then some of the circles become fragmented but can easily be traced to completion. Then further out there are ripples so disjointed it takes a greater effort of the active and excited imagination to link them and project their completion. Some stories are so powerfully suggestive that, even when the physical circles disappear, the pattern has been set and can be followed to infinity. This is the magic of the short story. The reader may enjoy the stunning experience of the first impression, may find satisfaction in the immediate complete circle of meaning, but by pursuing circle after circle he can travel far beyond the initial point of contact, can explore more and more layers of meaning, can end up chasing ideas that perhaps lie beyond the very grasp of reason.

The short story reader is always an active participant in the search, always seeking the horizon. He may never reach that destination, but what he learns along the way will make the journey worthwhile. Demands are made on him, work, effort, application, constant vigilance, and that is the reason why the short story is not popular with the masses who want only a little diverting entertainment on a commuter journey. No, the short story is akin to the poem: there is no facile satisfaction. Its appeal is to the imagination, and the imagination is insatiable. You can feed it, yes, but the more you feed it, the hungrier it becomes. On the other hand, the rational mind can be well satisfied with a five-course novel followed by brandy and cigar.

- *What about the problem of length?*

- That old chestnut! I think Poe hit the bullseye when he declared that a short story had to be perused at the one sitting. I know that it gave rise to a thousand and one jokes, including that Poe was measuring the length of the story by the durability of his backside. But Poe had a wonderful intuitive grasp of the true nature and the possibilities of the genre. If you consider all I have said, it is clear that the reading of a short story must be a single experience. In the oral tradition people would listen to the most complex and layered story, then go off, usually in awe, and let it reverberate in their minds. Similarly a short story must be read, must be ingested as a single object, even though the digestion of it is ruminatory. You can't deliver a hand-grenade in instalments.

- Do you think that layers of meaning are necessary in all stories?

- I would hope to be the last person to say what a short story should or should not do. I believe in the infinite possibility of the form. A story can set out to solve the riddle of the pyramids in an oblique way; it can explore a symbolic parallel between a medieval castle in an urban setting and the human head encasing the primitive psyche; it can do a million and one things. As a reader I expect a short story to challenge my imagination, to stir my sense of wonder. That might be achieved through subtlety of language, patterning of imagery, novelty of plot, characterisation, psychological insight, exploration of a symbol, whatever. I do expect to sense a mystery at the heart of every short story, and I do expect that that mystery will yield of its riches only very reluctantly and only after effort on my part. If a story has nothing to give but its face value, or if it yields its mystery too easily, it may still be a short story but a banal one. This might sound as if I'm advocating obscurantism. I'm not. Far from it. Think of the reading of a short story as meeting a person for the first time. At first you form impressions from the physical appearance, the mannerisms, the style of conversation. Then from conversing you learn a little more of this person, his occupation, his hobbies, his family background perhaps. You can continue meeting that person every day for the rest of your life, and learn a little more from every conversation, but you will never know everything. That's why people are endlessly fascinating. And so it should be with a short story.

- Finally, what do you think is necessary to make the short story popular again?

- Popularity is a dubious aspiration. Banality rather than profundity might seem to provide the recipe for popular success. But God knows, the reader has been sated with a diet of banality over the last forty years, with the result that he has decided to look elsewhere for sustenance. And can you blame him? It is not popularity we should be seeking for the short story, but something more basic, an audience, a readership. It will of necessity be a select readership and will be lured only by the promise of artistic satisfaction, intellectual excitement. The esteem of the short story should be on a par with poetry. We should abandon the coat-tails of the novel, and align the short story with poetry. Even the presentation of stories should indicate that they are to be considered individually and with circumspection. Instead of seeking to have them published in massed print on the pages of broadsheets, or in paperback volumes that ape the appearance of novels, perhaps we should be presenting them in small volumes like poetry, volumes that would emphasise the individuality of each story. Then the reader might be encouraged to approach the short story with the same care, attention, effort, he expects to bring to the reading of a poem.

- *Thank you.*

- So what do you intend to do with this tape?

- *Transcribe it. Shape it into a dissertation. Present it to my course director, and hopefully gain a top grade.*

- Is that all? I had hoped it might help you write a good story.

- *Oh yes, and that too.*

The Great Silence

You are curious, my dear Zee, concerning the Great Silence that has fallen upon this island. Yes, it is true: in ten years not a single book has been published. This would have been an unusual occurrence had it happened in the most unlettered society on the globe; to have happened in the most lettered was indeed phenomenal.

You have more than a slight acquaintance with our literary history, Zee. Even your distant country did not escape the deluge of literature that emanated from Ireland in the years preceding the Great Silence. The scale of that deluge was best conveyed, I think, by the commentator who compared it to the Japanese industrial explosion back in the nineteen sixties; the Japanese excelled at technology and flooded the world markets with motor-cars, television sets, transistor radios; the Irish excelled at writing and, decades later, flooded the world with novels, poetry, stories, plays.

Ireland has always had an enigmatic relationship with its writers, going from one extreme to the other, either smothering them with adulation, or stifling them with censorious neglect. And this national characteristic is not of recent origin; it is to be found in the most distant reaches of the past, as I shall now illustrate for you.

Before writing was invented, the Irish were a nation of writers, if you will excuse the paradox. For thousands of years there were poets, historians, storytellers, composing away, day in day out. They had to memorise their own compositions and the compositions of all who went before them, and had to transmit them orally from one generation to the next to preserve them from oblivion. By the time the Christian missionaries introduced the craft of writing to the island in the Fifth Century, there was an absolute mountain of material ready to be committed to paper. And the whole nation tackled that job with enthusiasm. The wealthy and privileged classes played their part gamely. Each nobleman or landowner supported as many writers as he could; indeed it became a matter of prestige to do so: his status and public profile were determined by the number of writers he was supporting, as, in other civilisations, they might be determined by the number of cattle he possessed. The great national project grew in scale until, eventually, there were more people engaged in writing than there were working in the fields. As you can imagine, a disastrous economic collapse resulted. There was famine and civil strife. Everybody else blamed the writers and proposed that they all be put to the sword. A massacre seemed unavoidable. The wealthy and privileged classes disowned the writers, denounced them as parasites, claimed that they had been blackmailed into supporting them all along. In the darkest hour of their plight there emerged from the ranks of the writers an elderly influential scholar and holy man who, because of an earlier dispute about copyright, had been living in exile. He returned with the proposition that the problem could be solved other than by slaughtering the writers. The King was interested and went to meet him. Negotiations followed that must have been frank and friendly, as they say, but were also extremely thorough. The most comprehensive national agreement was drawn up and endorsed by both sides. It limited the number of writers to a manageable proportion of the population. The writers who remained were guaranteed security of employment by the wealthy classes, but their conditions were straitened and their privileges severely curtailed.

I have narrated this incident for you, Zee, to illustrate the extreme fluctuations in the fortunes of our writers; there are also interesting parallels between the crisis that arose then - the end of the Sixth Century - and that which led to the Great Silence in recent times.

To be brief, times passed, times in which the national occupation thrived and Irish writers were the wonder of the world, times in which the national occupation was so neglected that the writers were reduced to the level of common beggars. A couple of decades ago the profession began to undergo one of its phases of enormous expansion. Vast unemployment in agriculture and industry had left hundreds of thousands on the dole queue. A percentage of those took up writing, sponsored by employment schemes of the European Union. A favourable image of writing was projected by the media, and thousands more transferred over, to swap the stigma of being unemployed for the status of being a writer. The financial rewards had not been more attractive for a long time as a result of agreements negotiated by the Writers' Union. New publishing houses sprang up like mushrooms. Old publishing houses enjoyed the boom they had been awaiting for generations. Printing presses were working around the clock. Books were being issued and launched daily. The public relations people were busy too, for, as we all know, a book is nothing if not properly promoted. Such was the enthusiasm for this renaissance that people began to resign from secure jobs in order to devote themselves fully to the personal and national endeavour: teachers gave up teaching, civil servants resigned their secure posts, accountants abandoned their balance sheets. The specialisation was felt in other quarters too: the printers were so busy producing books that the parish committees found it impossible to have a set of raffle tickets printed. Most important of all, the public relations people began to neglect other clients in their quest for the riches and the glory that resulted from handling a successful writer. And promotion became more important and more competitive as new writers emerged with new books demanding their quarter-hour of public attention. Few people had the leisure time to read these books: the writers were too busy writing, the promoters too busy promoting, the printers too busy printing, and the diminishing number of readers could not possibly cope with the huge range of titles on offer. The result was that a writer's quality was judged solely on the impact of his public appearances, his success on television chat-shows, the frequency with which his name was mentioned by the gossip columnists. And because they had once more become the currency of prestige, they were once more beloved of the rich and privileged.

However, the home market soon became saturated with books; the home radio and television stations could interview no greater number of writers. So, the export drive began. Novels, collections of poems, stories, biographies, books of literary criticism, were poured into the markets of the world. Most countries could have survived the deluge of books were it not for the promotion campaigns. Irish writers were now monopolising the television screens and the radio airwaves of the whole world. Morning, noon, and night they were being interviewed, in studios, in their back gardens, in their sitting rooms. Their faces became more familiar to newspaper readers than those of prime ministers or fashion models. They were picking up whatever awards and prizes were not firmly pinned down by the native writers in each country. Universities began to specialise in the study of Irish literature to the exclusion of all other. The competition for broadcasting time became more intense everywhere as the drive to promote more and more Irish writers continued. Even politicians were ousted from their patrimony on prime-time television in order to provide more publicity for the writers.

As you can imagine, Zee, an enormous jealousy welled-up among the writers of the world; a resentment of immense proportion and virulence welled-up among the politicians too, the sportsmen, the opinion-mongers, the hordes of similar dispossessed who felt they were being deprived of their glory by these Irish scribblers. Ugly scenes occurred in television studios where eminent men-of-letters were jostled and punched by their rivals. Mobs of discontented politicians and redundant raconteurs massed outside radio stations threatening the life and limb of the next Irish writer who might dare to enter. Governments were lobbied fiercely for an embargo on Irish books. However, as the device of the embargo had been jettisoned with the removal of trade barriers, there was a great reluctance to interfere with the free movement of goods for fear of undermining international trade agreements.

But there is always a lawyer somewhere who will come up

with the solution to any problem, isn't there? Somewhere in the world some lawyer pointed out a sub-clause in the small print of the global trade agreements, which allowed a government to take whatever action it deemed necessary to protect its national culture, notwithstanding its commitment to maintain an open market. That was enough. One government after another imposed embargoes on books from Ireland. There were unseemly demonstrations of euphoria on the streets of all the great cities of the world. Bonfires were built and fuelled with all the Irish books that could be found; the blaze is said to have illuminated the darkness over half the earth.

Only the European Union could not join the general embargo: the treaties were scrutinised minutely, but there was nothing there which would allow any discrimination of any kind against a member country. After the world embargo, however, the deluge of Irish books flooding into Europe was ten times greater than it had been before, and the demand for publicity from the promotion teams increased a hundredfold. There were huge demonstrations on the streets of European capitals, led by intellectuals, politicians, poets, supported by racist youths with tight haircuts who broke windows and burned cars. Anarchy was threatening.

The European Commission debated the problem. They were used to dealing with the over-supply of commodities, and they had a ready solution - quotas. In future each country would be restricted to a quota in book production. Exceeding the quota would incur the severest financial penalties.

Once more scenes of euphoric delight celebrated the curtailment of Irish literary output. Again bonfires of books lit the skies, this time from the Baltic to the Mediterranean.

In Ireland the ruling brought utter desolation. The country was plunged into the darkest of depressions. Once more the old spectres raised their awful heads: anonymity, economic catastrophe, murderous rivalry for the minute helpings of recognition and reward that remained on offer.

The Chairperson of the Writers' Union was summoned to an emergency meeting with the Minister for Culture. They discussed the crisis over several days. Both were anxious to avoid the dangers that could result from indecisive leadership. And so, after the most heated negotiations, the two of them emerged to make a joint announcement to a packed press conference. Ireland had no alternative but to apply the quota imposed by the European Union. Taking the number of writers in the country and the number of books that could be published from then on, the fairest way of implementing the quota was to limit each writer to one book in his or her lifetime. And that was what had been decided.

"One book?"

"One book."

"One book!"

Such was the shocked response of the half-million writers in the country.

Then fell the Great Silence.

At first, it seems, all the writers continued working away as usual. Novels that had been in progress were being completed. Stories and poems were being added to collections that had already been accumulating. Research continued on biographies and works of scholarship.

There was much debate about the new arrangement. It was expected that some of the young impetuous writers would rush in with their books to steal the honour of being first. But, only one book for a whole lifetime - they held back, unsure of themselves. It was then expected that some of the older writers would lead the way, especially those who might not have been likely to produce more than the one book in any event. But they held back as well, daunted perhaps by the single, absolute, and final judgement that was awaiting each publication. Courses in editing became very popular, and manuals on syntax topped the bestseller lists for the first time ever.

The rules agreed with the Minister for Culture stipulated that books ready for publication would be lodged with the Ministry; they would be received, examined, and held in care by a special senior official, who would then arrange to have them offered at auction to publishers, not fewer than ten of them being offered at each auction - this latter clause having been inserted by the publishers, who feared they would inflate their costs by bidding against each other every time a single book became available.

Seven years passed, and not a single book was submitted for publication. Great tomes were being written, but were not yet ready. Smaller tomes were being re-written, but were not yet fully polished.

At the end of seven years a middle-aged writer, one of the cleverest in the country, announced that he was ready to lodge his book for publication. No one was surprised. He was at the peak of his powers: he was bound to have written a good book in seven years. Nevertheless, the event aroused widespread interest, and stimulated intense speculation. How large was the book? What was it about? What form did it take?

It was quite a national occasion the morning he made his way to the Ministry of Culture. There was an atmosphere of carnival among the crowds thronging the streets, who had turned out to witness the event. Television cameras and microphones projected at him from all angles. Interviewers kept blocking his way, firing questions at him.

"How big is your book?"

"Not big."

"What is it about?"

"It's about life. It's about heaven and earth and hell. It's about philosophy and theology and economics. I suppose you could say it is about everything."

"Were you restricted as a writer in having to say it all in one book?"

"Not at all."

The writer squeezed through the crowds and up the steps of the Ministry. The great doors opened and there was a rousing cheer from the crowd as he disappeared inside. Whether he came out again the same door nobody seemed to notice; they were all waiting for the senior official to give his press conference, and they were not disappointed.

He stood at the top of the steps, while reporters and photographers and cameras and microphones pressed forward, and he read his statement.

"I wish to confirm that on this day I have received a work

which the author has submitted for publication in book form. It is a work of fiction, a short story of approximately three thousand words. It has now been lodged in the vault of the Ministry and will be offered to publishers at auction as soon as another nine books are received. I am prohibited from giving further details, or from discussing it in any way. Thank you."

The reaction was one of utter bewilderment.

"A short story!"

"Three thousand words!"

" And he says he has said everything!"

It was expected that the stream of books would now begin to flow. But it was quite the contrary. None was submitted. Books were finished and ready, but now the authors were doubly unsure. Ruthless judgement was one thing, but a comparison of their work with this short story was more than the stoutest hearts could brave. Seven years he spent! One short story on which he was prepared to be judged! It had to be good! It had to be extraordinary! It had to have said everything! No one was prepared to place his work alongside that.

The great tomes that were finished weighed heavily around the necks of their begetters. Unfinished novels ground to a halt. Incomplete collections of poems and stories were dropped into bottom drawers or packed into boxes under beds. No one could compete with the short story lodged in the vault of the Ministry of Culture.

And so, my dear Zee, the Great Silence continues. It is now three years since the story was offered for publication, and not another submission has been made since then. The magnificent literary tradition seems to have finally run its course after thousands of years. This may seem of minor importance to you, Zee, from your vantage point looking over the Bosphorous at the vast continent of Asia teeming with anonymous millions. To us it is unthinkable that the end has come: as a nation, and as individuals, we cannot abide anonymity.

Murphy in the Underworld

Murphy in the Underworld

I T CAME AS A PLEASANT SURPRISE TO Murphy to find that he could leave Hades at all. And to be able to leave once a year – that certainly exceeded expectation.

'Eternity revolves in a circular course, just as time follows the course of a spiral,' the lecturer explained in the acclimatisation class. 'But here in Hades there is no gradual realisation of the cycle; there are no flowers to blossom, no birds to migrate, no natural appetites to punctuate your existence. Change is unknown here: each revolution of the circle is a perfect repetition of the previous one. But between the old circle and the new one, between the dragon's tail and the dragon's mouth, there is an intermission. For this one night, November Night, the laws of eternity and infinity lapse, and you are free to return to the world of time and place for its duration.'

Murphy pondered long and luxuriously on his visit to the Upperworld. At first he thought of it only in a general way, as an escape from the grey monotony of the Caverns up to the blue sky and the green fields. Then his thoughts became more specific as he remembered the little village in the West of Ireland where he was born and reared, its cottages with their cobbled yards and a dung pit at every stable door, the bleak hills around the village straddled by meagre stone walls. It would be nice to see his mother again. He had not seen her for about ten years before he died, but he had written to her (and sent her a ten-pound note) every Christmas.

It would also be nice, he mused, to visit his mates in London, to have a stroll around the edge of Clapham Common, buy a packet of cigarettes in Oldtown, as was his custom, and drop down to the Alex for a few pints. Except that he had no use for cigarettes or pints anymore!

Murphy wondered whether it was possible to visit two places on the one night, or if he needed a special permit to do that. It was a pity he hadn't thought of asking the lecturer in the acclimatisation class. But it should be easy enough to get such information.

He enquired casually among the millions of souls that thronged the Caverns of Hades, but everyone he spoke to was apathetic and irritable. Finally, someone suggested that he ask in the Information Office of the Administration Wing. Murphy didn't like the sound of that. The few times he had visited the Tax Office in London, his experiences had instilled in him an inclination to avoid such places at all costs. But, when further questioning of his fellow-souls had failed to enlighten him, Murphy decided, against all his better prejudice, to enter the Administration Wing. Besides, what else was there to do in Hades?

His first glimpse of the Administration Wing was an awesome sight. It was an extension off the Main Cavern of Hades. But what an extension! A long corridor stretched out into the distance, possibly into infinity, and off that corridor were thousands of smaller ones, each studded with doors to individual offices. It was truly a labyrinth of immense proportions. But everywhere was stamped the message that its purpose was not to baffle, but to serve.

There were signs and arrows, pointers and notices, all to assist in the efficient conduct of the business of Hades. Murphy studied the signs: 'First Applications', 'Registrations', 'Renewed Applications', 'Personnel', 'Private, Staff Only', 'Information'. That was his one! He followed the pointers for 'Information' down the Central Corridor, into a side-corridor, around several corners, and eventually arrived at a door with the sign in bold letters staring dauntingly at him.

He knocked timidly on the door. There was no reply. Perhaps they're gone to lunch, thought Murphy in relief. Then he remembered that there was no such thing as lunch in Hades. He opened the door cautiously. Inside was a long partition with a series of hatches built into it. A notice ordered: 'Ring bell for service.' Murphy rang the bell.

A hatch slammed open, reminding Murphy vaguely of a confessional box. A sombre-looking soul peered out at him.

'I'm new here,' explained Murphy, 'and I wanted to get some information on the passes for November Night. You see, I'd like to visit two places that night, if I could. I'd like to go home to Ireland, but I'd also like to make the trip to London.'

'Have you filled in an application form?' boomed the voice through the hatch.

'No. Not yet,' replied Murphy.

'The first thing you must do is fill in an application form.'

'Righto. I'll do that. Thanks,' said Murphy, glad that that little matter had been disposed of so easily.

He made his way back to the Central Corridor and started looking for a sign, 'First Applications', that he had noticed earlier. Eventually he spotted it and followed carefully from one arrow to another until he arrived in a huge office with multitudes queuing at each hatch. Murphy took his place in one of the queues.

Progress towards the hatch was slow and tedious, but Murphy was preoccupied with his dreams of the Upperworld. He would visit Ireland first. It would probably be dusk when he got there, with the house-lights beginning to wink from the side of the mountain. His mother would be inside their cottage, pulling the curtains, heaping turf on the fire, wetting a pot of tea. She might not have heard of his death - there was no one who would have known to tell her. It would be nice if she thought he was still alive, because he was really; at least he didn't feel any different. And then he would travel down towards London through Dublin and Holyhead, past the slagheaps of Wales, just as if he were on the night train to Euston.

Eventually Murphy reached the top of the queue. He asked for an application form, explaining the peculiarity of his wishes.

The official shook his head. 'You're in the wrong office. You need to go to the "Special Applications" section and ask for Form D.23.'

Murphy felt frustrated, especially after spending so long in the queue. But there was no point in getting angry. So he trudged back to the Central Corridor and began searching again. A great weariness oppressed him. Then he realised: how could he feel weary when he had no body? It must be psychological, he concluded; everything was bloody-well psychological anymore.

After scouring the Central Corridor for a long while he saw a pointer for 'Special Applications', and after a further lengthy quest he discovered the office.

'I would like to fill in Form D.23,' Murphy intimated to the clerk behind the hatch, when he got to the top of that queue. 'You see, I would like to visit two places on November Night, my home in Ireland, and London where I used to work.'

'I'm afraid D.23 is not the correct form for you. This form is an application for spatial immunity. It's for someone who wants to visit no individual place, but the earth in general, covering all places at once. Now what you must do is this. You must go to "First Applications" and fill in two forms, one for each of the two places you wish to visit.'

So Murphy proceeded on his pilgrimage. A weak but indigenous voice inside him began to whisper that he should run, run until he was well clear of office and desk and clerk; but he silenced that voice ruthlessly, riveting his thoughts to the little village on the shores of the Atlantic.

It was again a long tedious affair getting through the queue in the 'First Applications' section. But Murphy made it at last. 'I would like two forms to fill in, please,' said he to the clerk.

'Nobody gets two forms,' declared the clerk with a slow, deliberate and absolute shake of his head. Murphy gave up in despair.

When he emerged from the Administration Wing into the Main Cavern of Hades, he threw himself down dejectedly along the wall and sat brooding.

'It will be November Night shortly,' said a soul, who was sitting near him, more to himself than to Murphy.

'What!' exclaimed Murphy. 'It couldn't be!'

'It's as near as dam'it,' said the other.

'My God, the time flies down here,' gasped Murphy.

The other soul glanced at him curiously. 'Are you just over?' he asked.

Either he didn't understand the language in which Murphy phrased the subsequent remarks, or else they reached a level of obscenity which was far beneath his plumb, but he watched Murphy with the same curious expression as the latter stalked off muttering: 'No matter where you go, there's some bastard who got there before you and thinks he owns the shagging joint.'

Murphy had not gone far when he felt a transformation taking place. He suddenly sensed that the shackles were falling away, as if he were being released from all limitation. Instinctively he knew that he was free of Hades. It all came so naturally to him that it took him by surprise. He knew that one act of will was all that was required to take him to his mother's cottage in Ireland. He willed it, and he was there. His first thought on reaching the Upperworld was: 'What was all that bullshit about passes?'

* * *

The jurisdiction of Hades returned with the dawn. Murphy had not succeeded in getting to London. Not that he wasn't able! On the contrary, he experienced total freedom of movement. But when he got to his mother's cottage he found it dark and uninhabited. It looked as if nobody had lived there for years. But where could she be? He searched the neighbours' houses. He went around on all his relatives, eavesdropping on their conversations, but not a trace of her could he find anywhere. He searched vainly until morning when he felt the pull of Hades upon him again.

Could she have died? Surely someone would have told him.

But then, who could have told him? He hadn't talked with anyone from home for many years, and, with the way he changed his digs every second week, his mother never knew his address. If she were dead, she would be here in Hades and he could find her.

Murphy looked about the Cavern. For the first time he realised the significance of the fact that souls had no distinguishing features as bodies had. Each looked exactly like the next; so any one of the souls in front of him could be his mother and he wouldn't know. He would have to speak to each of them to discover its identity. And Murphy had already found that souls were reluctant to talk at all. They were totally self-centred, brooding forever on their former lives.

There were countless millions of souls in Hades, and to find his mother he would have to interview each one of them in turn. That would be an impossible task, even with all the time he had at his disposal (or, as he should say, even with all eternity at his disposal - he would have to stop using these 'temporalisms' as the lecturer called them; they gave him away as a newcomer).

'What about that vast Administration?' he thought. 'They must have some record of who comes in.'

But Murphy wasn't going to go through the same mill he had gone through before. He had often heard his mates in London claim that the best method of dealing with large offices was to ask for the man in charge. It was no use talking to the clerk: he tried to get rid of you; but ask for the man in charge and you had them all shitting in their trousers (that was another custom that became extinct on entering Hades!).

So he made his way to the Information Office again. He asked for the soul in charge and was ushered into a room that had the sign 'Superintendent' on the door.

Behind the desk sat the Superintendent who asked, without curiosity, what his problem was.

'It's like this,' began Murphy. 'On the night-off there I went back home. I was looking for my mother, but I couldn't find her anywhere. So I thought that maybe she was down here. I'm wondering if there is any way I can find out.'

'We do keep a record of all who are admitted,' replied the Superintendent. 'But unfortunately, due to shortage of staff, we have not yet been able to file the admission cards in any kind of order. If you wish you may go through the cards. However, it would probably be more advisable to search for herself. You see, even if you came across her card it would only confirm that she was here, it would be of no assistance in finding her.'

Murphy could not contain his irritation. 'What's the bloody use of this infernal Civil Service if you can't do something as simple as check if my mother is here? It's all bullshit as far as I can see. I spent the best part of a year queuing up to get a pass for November Night, and when the time came I found that I was able to go off without any pass at all.'

'You went to the Upperworld without a pass!' cried the Superintendent rising in horror off his seat. 'I see now that it's one of these anarchists I'm dealing with. Trying to destroy everything we have achieved! But you won't succeed, you won't succeed! Order will always triumph over the forces of disorder.'

'It's not much of an achievement, just to convince people they need something that they don't need at all. Any con-man could do that. So what are you making such a big deal out of it for?'

'The procedure of issuing passes for November Night is the basis of our whole Administration,' said the Superintendent, getting tensely emotional, 'and the Administration is the one thing that gives order and meaning to life in Hades. You anarchists will sneer at us, you will try to subvert our credibility. But we have succeeded in spite of you. Look at this wall-chart here. This is a blueprint for the future expansion of Hades. It is designed to cope with any possible increase in the rate of admission. Note that the Administration Corridor is going to replace the Main Cavern as the focal point of the Underworld. See how all future developments are going to radiate from the Administration Corridor in a grid pattern. That's what order and progress are about. That's what you're undermining when you go to the Upperworld without a pass.'

'As far as I'm concerned you can stick your order and progress up your ...' Murphy checked himself against the use of a temporalism. 'Since there's nothing you can do for me I'll go and start searching for my mother.' Murphy moved towards the door.

'The rules are that you cannot go around annoying souls in any of the main caverns or in the new sections,' said the Superintendent, coming after him.

'Where am I supposed to look then?' asked Murphy angrily.

'The Lost Souls' Section,' replied the Superintendent. 'It's a designated area of Old Hades. It may be a comfort to you,' he put as much sarcasm as he could into these words, 'to know that about ninety percent of your nation is down there already. Along with other undesirable qualities, they bring their ghetto-mentality with them.'

For the first time since he entered Hades, Murphy experienced something approaching joy. The idea of an Irish settlement in the Underworld warmed him to the core. He couldn't wait to find it.

He hurried back to the Main Cavern and proceeded in the direction of Old Hades. When he had travelled a distance he noticed that the throngs were getting thinner and thinner. Eventually he heard a hum in the distance, a low steady hum. The further he went, the louder the hum became, until it reached a deafening intensity. Then, rounding a corner he saw, stretched out before him, the Lost Souls' Section of Hades.

There were myriads of souls, mingling restlessly, crying out in loud voices, shouting names, asking questions, millions of them in perpetual motion like water-beads in a turbulent seething ocean.

Murphy gazed at this pitiable sight. 'Finding someone in that melee,' he thought, 'must be at greater odds than winning the Pools.' He saw, within the swirl, two souls meet, identify, embrace, cling to each other lest they be separated by the next swell and be lost again for all eternity. But for the two that met there were millions who were still searching.

Perhaps his mother wasn't there at all. She might have chosen to remain in the relative peace of the other Caverns. For all he knew, she mightn't even be dead yet. Wouldn't he be a right mug if he was going around screaming her name in this infernal din, and she still up above, drinking a bottle of stout, maybe?

But what else was there to do? He listened intently to the babble. He could distinguish many shades of Irish dialect from Dublin to Donegal, from Kerry to Sligo, interspersed with an occasional phrase uttered in a strange language. And far away, Murphy could swear he heard someone singing in a drunken drawl:

> *Come back, Paddy Reilly, to Ballyjamesduff,*
> *Come home, Paddy Reilly, to me.*

He remembered all the people from home that had died; they would all be in there; so would all the men he had worked with in England. Even if he didn't find his mother, he might meet someone he knew; and even if he didn't meet anyone he knew, he would surely have the odd good chat.

So Murphy plunged into that sea of restless souls and began shouting and questioning like the rest of them. Then he was suddenly arrested by a curious thought: he wondered whether this was heaven or hell. But a moment's reflection convinced him of the irrelevance of that question, and he resumed calling out his mother's name among the lost souls of Hades.

Come Follow Me

BONAPARTE LANE WAS A BACK STREET IN our neighbourhood off the great thoroughfare of Bonaparte Avenue. It is a rundown deserted place now, but when I was ten years old it housed a lively community of a dozen families or more. Few streets, or families, experience the finality of a 'Last Day', but on one dark evening in November Bonaparte Lane ceased to exist as a community.

I witnessed that climax, that catastrophe, so I feel I am better qualified than most to chronicle the events that caused it.

Bonaparte Lane had a reputation of legendary proportion all over our city for the excellence of card-playing that could be witnessed nightly in all its houses. The best players from every quarter of the city would converge on the little lane to try their skills and their intelligence against the citizens of this revered street. For someone who was learning the art of card-playing, it was a big moment in his life when he felt ready for his first visit to so awe-inspiring an arena. Fathers, around the family card-table, would encourage their young sons by saying: 'You'll soon be fit for Bonaparte Lane.' Or, if any slovenly play was detected at a card-game in a distant quarter of the city someone might comment: 'If they had you in Bonaparte Lane, they'd throw you in the river' - a reference to the woefully polluted stream that intersected the Lane at the bottom end.

Slovenly play was never tolerated at the card-tables in the Lane. If anyone were found to be cheating or trying to cheat, play would cease immediately, and the offender would be asked to leave the house; a person thus disgraced would not be permitted to sit down to a card-table in Bonaparte Lane for the rest of his life.

Gambling was outlawed as ruthlessly as cheating and there was never so much as a penny staked on any game in the Lane. There were those who thought this policy short-sighted, because the men, women, and children of the street were brilliantly skillful at cards and if they took to playing for stakes they could have reduced the rest of the city to beggary.

Tradition was deeply rooted in the little community. The ethics and standards governing their card-playing were handed down to them along with the skills over many generations. And so they regarded themselves as the custodians of these ethics and these skills, singled out as a kind of chosen people, a race apart. Saturday nights were reserved for playing exclusively among themselves, but often outsiders came just to watch these games and to observe card-playing at its very best.

One day - it was either in the late spring or early summer - a sailor staggered into the entry and asked the children playing there where the 'casino' was. Naturally enough, they stared at the intoxicated seaman uncomprehendingly. Quickly recognising their confusion, he took a pack of cards out of his pocket and brandished them wildly over his head.

'Where do they play cards?' he asked in the rhythmless voice of one who has had to learn the language.

The children's faces lit up on recognising the familiar object.

'In every house,' came their chorus of reply.

'Which is the best house?' asked the sailor.

The children were again perplexed. They looked around and saw me standing a short distance away. I was a little older than they, so they looked pleadingly to me to resolve the problem. The way I reasoned it, one house was as good as the next, but the only house in which he would be welcome at that hour of the day was Alex Bryce's. Alex lived alone and spent most of the day in bed or lounging about, so he was always happy to have someone call in. I directed the sailor towards Alex's house, and watched him totter down the footpath and disappear through the perennially open door.

Bonaparte Lane was never the same again. The sailor turned out to be not only gifted as a player but also adept at every type of game. Heretofore, different individuals were champions and undisputed masters of certain games; but within a week the sailor had challenged and defeated each master at his own game. The citizens of the Lane rallied against this threat to their supremacy. All day and all evening they plotted and devised strategies; all night they pitted their knowledge and cunning against the foreign sailor in game after game. But the sailor disposed of each challenge with the ease and competence of one who was merely engaging in some preliminary exercises. When it finally became evident that he was never going to be beaten, a depression set in over the whole community. People gathered, as if by force of custom, at their usual rendezvous points but no one was interested in playing cards. It was not the fact of being beaten that disheartened the people - they had often experienced defeat before, on an individual basis - it was the fact that one man could take on the whole Lane, with its wealth of expertise, and win. It shook their confidence. It raised a question mark over their faith in the superiority conferred on them by tradition.

The sailor had taken up lodgings in Alex Bryce's and seemed in no hurry to return to sea. When the visitors at night declined his invitation to play cards he grew morose and sent for whiskey. While he swallowed the liquor straight from the bottle he shuffled the pack of cards and dealt them out in various patterns, muttering to himself in his own language.

Then one night, when the visitors arrived, they found the sailor sober and excited. He had the table pulled into the middle of the floor and set ready for a card-game.

'Sit down! Sit down!' cried he. 'And I will teach you some new games. I have many games that I learned in Rio de Janeiro, and Port Said, and Casablanca.'

They reluctantly took their seats. The sailor deftly shuffled the pack and flicked the cards to all who were seated.

'This game is called "Cinch",' said he, and proceeded to outline the rules of the game. The visitors warmed to the idea of learning a new game and quickly mastered it. Then the sailor went on to instruct them in "Fan Tan".

The following night almost everyone from the Lane crowded into Alex Bryce's house to learn the new games from the sailor.

They were enthusiastic about some of the games that demanded skill, intelligence, concentration; but they were apathetic about others that demanded nothing of the player but proceeded mechanically toward an outcome determined by haphazard luck.

The sailor had a vast repertoire of card-games and after three weeks he was still demonstrating new ones.

Then one night, while interest was still high, he asked loudly: 'Can anyone read the cards?'

An instantaneous silence descended on the room. The people of Bonaparte Lane were very wary of that aspect of cards and never dabbled in it, either in earnest or in fun.

'Come, come, it is only another game,' enticed the sailor. 'Cut the cards and we will find out which of the ladies dreams of a lover. The secrets of the mind revealed! Who will cut the cards?'

He started to shuffle the pack. A woman at the door coughed, muttered a goodnight, and made her way out. She was followed by another, and soon all the women were leaving, herding their youngsters in front of them.

But the men stayed, and it evidently proved to be the most engaging of all demonstrations because not one of them stirred out of the house until three in the morning. And the following evening, as they ate a hurried dinner, the men were full of wonder and admiration and excitement.

Because I was little more than a child at the time I heard nothing of what was going on at the sailor's card-table during the following nights. All discussion about it among the adults was carried on in huddled groups. The women were anxious and edgy and were in no humour for casual conversations with a youngster from a neighbouring street.

The days went by and the men became more reticent and more involved. Often they stayed at cards so late that some of them were not able to rise for work the following morning. Eventually one man stopped going to work altogether, then another, until finally there wasn't a man in the whole Lane who was holding a regular job. This left them free to start into the cards as soon as they cleared the sleep out of their eyes and had eaten whatever meagre breakfast was provided by their disaffected wives.

The strangest protest against what was happening in Bonaparte Lane was made by the priest. Some said he recognised the Devil's handiwork when he heard of the card-playing; others held that he had nearly exploded when he found a 'nil' return from the Lane in the Church collection. He appeared in the entry one day fully robed as if he were going to say Mass, walked down the Lane, and stopped outside Alex Bryce's. He took out his breviary and started to recite prayers in an incomprehensible murmur. Every now and again he would raise his right hand in a gesture towards the sky. He spent at least half-an-hour in the middle of the street, watched by three or four women, a lot of curious children, and a few dogs, and when he had finished he departed as enigmatically as he had come, without a word of explanation. Some held the opinion that he was putting his curse on the house. One woman suggested that he might have been praying for the souls of the men within, but she was contradicted flatly by the rest who declared that, whatever he was doing, his tone was not appropriate to praying. There was no indication from the house that the men were aware of the incident in the street outside; at least if they were so aware they did not stop play even to look out the window.

Gradually a severe poverty began to afflict the families in the Lane. Objects of value were pawned to put food on the table. The tyres of the car outside Murnaghan's went flat, the chassis rusted, and the engine seized; what had been a family car was now a derelict. The rounds of the St. Vincent de Paul man took on a major importance in the life of this formerly prosperous little street.

One evening around tea time I was sitting underneath Newmans' window. I happened to overhear part of an argument between Martin Newman and his wife. It was the only hint I ever got of what was going on at Alex Bryce's card-table, and even that hint wasn't very enlightening.

'Where is it all leading to?' asked Mrs. Newman in a slightly demented tone. 'What do you expect to find out?'

'It's not what you find out at the end of the journey that's important,' replied Martin, 'It's what you learn along the way. The cards represent the whole world. Right? When they're laid out in different patterns and different combinations, it's amazing how much they tell you about life. Yet, no matter how much you learn, you feel you are about to understand something far more important. Only it keeps eluding you like the horizon or the rainbow's end.'

'Your family is on the brink of starvation. You have no job, nor the prospect of one. And you want to learn about life from a pack of cards. It's above in the asylum the lot of you should be.'

'Will you hold your tongue, woman,' shouted Martin. 'There are higher things in life than jobs and food. But you wouldn't appreciate that. Would you?'

A moment later he almost tripped over my legs in his haste down the street towards Alex Bryce's.

As the winter crept in and the weather became harder the predicament of the families worsened rapidly. Without fuel the houses were cold and damp. A flu epidemic had most of the children confined to bed. It was at that time that the women of the Lane gathered into Pearse's house where a year-old infant was ill with the flu. John Pearse, along with the other men, had already settled into the cards over in Bryce's house. His wife was nearly distracted with worry about the infant, and the other women were consoling her.

'When John comes home, you have a good chat with him,' said Mrs. Hynes. 'He's a good man, and when he sees how worried you are about the child he'll do something.'

'You're a silly woman, Mary Hynes,' declared Mrs. Newman. 'You don't understand. None of you does. You think that this is going to be over soon. You think that someday you'll wake up and it will all be behind you, like a bad nightmare. Well you're wrong. It will never be over. Never, I said. The men have gone their own way, searching for something. Mind you, they don't know what they're looking for, so I suppose they wouldn't recognise it even if they found it. But they have forgotten about their responsibilities. They no longer feel any obligations to us or to the children. I can see from your faces that you don't believe me. Or maybe you don't want to believe me but that a voice inside you is whispering that I'm right. I am right. And I'll prove I'm right. Do you all agree that John Pearse was as good and as kind a man as ever walked down Bonaparte Lane?'

There was a general nodding of assent.

'Mollie,' she said gently to Mrs. Pearse. 'Can I have your permission to send a message over to John to say that the baby is dying and that he had better come at once. Now if he refuses to come on a summons like that, and I think he will refuse, it will prove my point.'

Mrs. Pearse nodded slowly and bit on her lower lip.

Mrs. Newman turned around and eyed me standing just inside the door.

'Cornelius,' she called. 'You bring the message over to John Pearse. Tell him that his baby is dying and that he is needed urgently at home. Tell him that, and tell him nothing more.'

I didn't like the job I was given, but such was the atmosphere in the house that I didn't even contemplate refusing. I went outside and crossed the street. The place was deserted and so quiet I imagined the tapping of my crutches echoed from one end of the Lane to the other. Up the three granite steps I advanced tremulously. The door to the living room opened without a creak, and I stepped into the preoccupied silence within. Momentarily I stood unnoticed inside the door. The sailor was sitting at the centre of the table and the rest of the men were gathered around it, like those pictures of Christ and his disciples at the Last Supper.

Then Alex Bryce looked up from the table and noticed me. The others turned around.

'Well, Cornelius,' said Alex. 'What are you doing here?'

'I have a message for John Pearse,' said I. 'His baby is dying and he's wanted at home.' I blurted out my message abruptly and noticed the immediate impression of shock it created on the men's faces. Silent, motionless, they stared one at another. It was as if a moment they had long awaited had finally arrived.

No one replied to me, so I withdrew from the room and made my way back across the empty street. Inside Pearse's front door again I opened my mouth to report the completion of my mission, but it was obvious from the faces there that I didn't have to say anything. They were waiting now.

The silence in that living-room was deathly, but very real, palpable. All the women stared fixedly at something in front of them, the corner of the table, the flame of the Sacred Heart lamp, or the empty fire-grate.

The children could be heard coughing in the bedroom upstairs. In the distance the lonely sound of a ship's horn hooted out over the city. Seconds plodded by as if they were retarded with weights of lead.

There was no sign of activity in the house across the street. Not a curtain flickered; not a shadow darkened the open door.

After half-an-hour Mrs. Newman broke the silence. 'We'll give him until ten-past-eight. That's a full hour from the time we sent the message.'

Nobody else opened a mouth, and the utter silence re-enveloped the room. Minute followed agonising minute.

Mrs. Pearse began to weep quietly and Mrs. Newman put an arm around her shoulders. But no one else moved. They were too preoccupied with their own pain. For they recognised that this was their tragedy as well as Mrs. Pearse's. If her husband would not come to her on such an awesome bidding, then no husband would answer any summons.

As soon as the clock turned ten-past-eight, the women shook themselves and began to get up quietly, as if a hypnotist had clicked his fingers to waken them from a trance. There was a clarity about them also, a suggestion that they were confronting a harsh reality with cold awareness, a feeling that the trance and the dream had been absolutely dispelled.

They each left without saying a word, and proceeded to their own houses. There they gathered together their children, blankets, clothes, and whatever food they had. And each woman left her home, turned her back on Bonaparte Lane, and set out for some other quarter of the city. By midnight there wasn't a woman or child left in the Lane.

I saw very few of them afterwards. Some went to their parents, some to relatives, some to institutions of one kind or another. But none of them ever returned to their homes in Bonaparte Lane.

IN THE
RETIREMENT COLONY

On his retirement from the position of senior architect in the Building Corporation, Albert Maloney was dispatched with his wife and chattels to the Grade 1 Resort of K on the South-East Coast. In tribute to the position he had attained on the occupational scale, he was given a detached house (No. 9830) with a modest garden front and rear.

The agent who met them and introduced them to their new home stressed the quietness of the neighbourhood, the short walk to the seafront, the proximity of amenities, and the remove of the Grade 2 Resort. But Albert noted, with satisfaction, how little the surroundings differed from the suburbs they had left; there were rows of secluded houses, each with its neatly-kept rose garden. He could not fault the house he was given either; it was more than adequate. Houses were allotted according to rank, and the allotment did not take into account the needs of the occupants. So, according to the order of things, Albert and his wife found themselves with a five-bedroom house.

On the following day they were visited by two members of the Residents' Committee who welcomed them to the resort and described the whole range of pastimes and sports that was open to them. They then brought Albert and his wife outside and introduced them to Mr and Mrs 9829 and Mr and Mrs 9831.

It was a smooth transition and Albert was soon settled into a routine of bowling in the morning, a little golf in the afternoon, a walk along the seafront in the evening with Mrs Albert followed by a few drinks at the club. His wife quickly became assimilated into the life of the Retirement Colony likewise: she became involved in a round of coffee mornings, and (in the absence of charity committees to work for) the ladies knitted and sewed items of dress for each other.

In accordance with the rationale of the Great Plan, people enjoyed the quality of retirement they had earned as workers. And Albert had worked hard. For forty years he had sat before a drawing-board designing public toilets, council houses, recreation centres, libraries, office blocks; for forty years he had driven to the office in the early morning and driven home from the office in the late evening; for forty years he had watched television five nights a week and indulged in gentle social intercourse at the weekends. For forty years he had held before his mind the prospect of a luxury retirement in a Grade 1 Resort. And his life had been a total success.

Albert had no interest in gardening, but his wife thought that he ought to cultivate a rose-bed or, at least, keep the hedges trim. All the other husbands took pride in their gardens and Mrs Albert did not wish to be embarrassed before her friends. So she asked the horticultural adviser to call on Albert. Twice the adviser called but found no one at home. The next time he called, he caught Albert making an earlier-than-usual expedition to the bowling green.

Albert cursed his luck, in his own quiet way, but listened respectfully to the adviser's monologue on soil nutrition, environmental improvement, rotation of crops, etc., etc.; but all he could remember, when the adviser had gone, was: 'What you need is topsoil, plenty of topsoil.' That encounter left Albert depressed all day. He felt he was now obliged to make some token effort. Back in the city he had always hired a casual gardener one day each fortnight to take care of his hedge and lawn. But that wasn't possible here; here everyone was retired, and all the retired workmen were over in the Grade 2 Resort.

Day followed day, and Albert soon forgot about the garden and the horticultural adviser. It was more difficult to induce oblivion to the ever-present stimulus of his wife's nagging, but he was so content with his pastimes that no care could occupy the vacancy of his mind for very long.

His retirement stretched out before Albert like a placid ocean that is almost too indolent to reflect the sun. But the placidity of the ocean is convulsed by the onslaught of a sudden storm. And the peace of Albert's life was similarly rocked by something as inconsequential as a dream.

It was not an exceptional dream. With his father and brothers he was building a pyramid, not even an ornate pyramid - like the ones in Guatemala - just a regular Egyptian-style pyramid. They were constructing it from cut limestone, carrying each block on a litter up a steep ramp. Working, and sweating, and grunting, they lodged stone upon stone and the pyramid was very close to completion. It was a gigantic structure and each time they descended to the ground for another block, they paused to look up at it with silent pride.

That was the full extent of the dream but it left Albert's mind in a state of intense agitation. Childhood memories and obscure longings arose from remote corners of his soul. He remembered his father building a shed at the back of their house in the long twilit evenings of a distant summer. He remembered his brothers picking potatoes when November frost had stiffened the clay. He remembered the delicious sweat that lathered his face when they were working furiously at the hay to rescue it from the weather.

The morning after his dream Albert lay in bed for a long while. The time for his bowling came and went. The time for his lunch passed. The time for his trip to the golf course arrived, but Albert continued to lie in bed, remembering. It was evening when he eventually arose, much to the relief of Mrs Albert who had been contemplating summoning a doctor. But he went about the house in an air of remoteness as if he had lost touch with his surroundings.

The pyramid that he and his family were building preoccupied Albert for many days thereafter. He forgot about his bowling and his golf, and stayed indoors meditating the structure, mentally gauging stress and thrust. Eventually he took down his drawing-board and began to make sketches of the pyramid as he remembered it. When the sketches were finished he started detailed drawings based on his own experience and knowledge of architecture.

Day after day Albert remained indoors poring over his drawings, and the more he progressed, the more he marveled at the ingenuity of the ancient builders. Sometimes they situated a pyramid to encompass a hill; it cut down on filling; and their calculations could be trusted to produce total symmetry in the end. What labour to lay that solid square! What thousands of slaves it took to lift it from the earth! With what indignation the captive tribes of Israel raised those soaring triangles! Soaring towards what? Towards the apex and the centre! Towards unity and perfection! Towards a monumental image of life and a symbol of death!

Mrs Albert's anxiety was fanned to panic by her husband's strange behaviour. He had never before acted in an unpredictable way. Without doubt he was unwell; yet he would not admit her to the room to ascertain his temperature; nor would he accept his customary mild laxative. She invited some of his friends from the golf club to come and speak to him, but they tapped fruitlessly on the room door.

How glorious for an architect to design and construct a building which transcends the mundane, the trivial! What a waste was his own life, thought Albert. The dream revealed it all. He should have worked with his own people. Triangle over square! Together they could have raised a monumental image of life, a symbol of death.

Albert cursed the order of things that had decreed his separation from his people. One house, one shed built out of that relationship would have been worth more than all the office blocks and libraries he had ever designed. Now it was too late. Now he was in the Grade 1 Resort enjoying the quality of retirement he had earned as a senior official of the Building Corporation.

Disillusion and depression became intense. Albert's only joy now was his reveries of childhood. They were always memories of work, but work performed in an emotional environment. That was what was lacking in his life since then - an emotional environment. He longed to be re-united with his family; he longed for the security of his father's affection, his brothers' prowess; he longed to perform even one act in communion with them. But they were all in the Grade 2 Resort.

Albert started walking abroad again, taking a particular interest in the monstrous dividing wall between the Grade 1 Resort and the Grade 2 Resort. He studied the rows of spikes that continued the division out into the sea. When he swam out from shore he saw the overcrowded beach on the other side of the wall; there were thousands of people hustling and jostling for room; cheap food vendors' stalls lined the short untidy promenade. When he climbed the hill beyond the rows of houses he could see over the wall; he saw the high-rise flats which might have been constructed from one of his own blueprints; he saw the people going to-and-fro on the open landings in unbelievable numbers; he saw the paltry courtyards which seemed to be the only amenity areas in the whole scheme.

Conditions in the Grade 2 Resort were obviously deplorable. Two weeks previously Albert would have been repelled by the sight or even the thought of such squalor. Now, because of his dream, he felt differently. A strong feeling of affinity with this bustling mass had established itself firmly in his heart.

It was not possible to travel from the Grade 1 Resort to the Grade 2 Resort, Albert was informed by the estate agent, the only official he could find in the whole Retirement Colony. But Albert was determined to visit the Grade 2 Resort nevertheless. He could not go over the wall, nor around it - so he would have to go under it! A tunnel from his back garden - topsoil, plenty of topsoil. His course was settled: he would drive a tunnel from his own garden, from inside his garden shed, under the dividing wall and into the Grade 2 Resort.

Mrs Albert was greatly relieved on seeing her husband out and about again, and she resumed her daily routine. She was even more pleased when she heard that he was going to start gardening.

Albert surveyed the route the tunnel would take, and from his vantage point on top of the hill he planned exactly where he would surface on the other side of the wall. On the pretext that

In the Retirement Colony

he was going to start digging the garden and repairing the garden shed, he purchased a pick, spade, shovel, crow-bar, sledgehammer, saw, and timber beams.

Before he could begin to tunnel he had to dig the garden, so that he could spread out the excavated soil. Then he started to sink a vertical shaft from inside the shed. He had no fear of discovery as his wife never came into the garden. She fluttered her fingers at him whenever she was passing between the front door and the gate. Once, she paused to inquire what type of flower he was planting, but she was quite content when she could chatter securely to her friends about her husband's newly-found passion for gardening.

When his wife was away from home in the morning and in the afternoon, Albert worked on the tunnel; when she was at home he barrowed the clay from the shed into the garden and spread it out over the ground.

His hands blistered and hurt at first, but he didn't mind; he welcomed the appearance of brown welts at the base of his fingers, the disappearance of some of the soft pink flesh. What absence of personality those hands showed! Even his face - and Albert touched the skin that hung limply from his jawbones - showed no qualities of character. He was glad he had no children: he could never have left an impression on them, as adults had left on him when he was a child. He remembered an old uncle who used to smoke a pipe - he would rummage in his pocket and bring forth a crumpled matchbox smelling of sweat - his uncle's matchbox had more personality than had Albert's face. But now he was digging his way to those real people. He would start again. He would work and build. And that thought lent force to his pick.

On the rafters of the shed he fixed a pulley and used it to raise the bucket of clay to the surface. When he had reached a depth of fifteen feet he began to cut the horizontal shaft. He had to be careful now as the earth was soft. Every five feet he placed a pair of timber props and ran flat bars from one prop to another to support the weight of the roof. Progress was slow but Albert was in no hurry. He relished every hour he spent in the tunnel. It was the greatest undertaking of his life.

One afternoon the horticultural adviser was passing and he stopped when he saw Albert. He looked at the extra soil spread out over the garden and was visibly shocked. He scratched his forehead with rapid motions of his fingers and inquired where Albert got the soil. The reply was couched in the vaguest possible terms. 'You've been fleeced. That's not topsoil, that's the poorest quality subsoil. You wouldn't grow moss on that.' And Albert assured him that he would pursue the matter with his supplier and demand compensation.

It was a cause of great exultation when, according to his calculations, he had driven his tunnel under the dividing wall. The awareness that fifteen feet above him were his family and perhaps the vast majority of the people he had known as a child rippled gaily through his mind. Even the clay seemed warmer.

In the next few days he worked harder than before and soon reached the point where he was to ascend.

At ten o'clock on a Monday morning Albert commenced cutting the vertical exit shaft. Dumping the buckets of clay was a slow operation at this stage, but he estimated that the exit would be complete by the end of the week.

About an hour after he had started he heard a loud thud. Stunned by the shock of anticipated disaster, he crept back through the tunnel to find that there had been an extensive cave-in. The props had collapsed under the weight of the roof. It was just beneath the dividing wall. He had under-estimated the pressure of the wall.

Albert started shoveling away the fall-in. He had to clear a vent quickly or he would suffocate. For an hour he worked frantically but did not succeed in breaking through. When his breath came in deep jerking gasps he knew the air was used up. He threw aside the shovel and lay down. The heavy breathing was tearing at his lungs. Exhausted, he closed his eyes. Beads of sweat were running down his forehead. He looked around and saw that his father's brow also was lathered in sweat and that he too was panting under the great weight of the stone, which was placed closer to his end of the litter. They strained and stumbled up the ramp, higher and higher. Despite

In the Retirement Colony

their fatigue they were proud and full with a sense of purpose, for this was the final block of the pyramid, the coping-stone, the apex, and the centre.

The Bleeding Stone of Knockaculleen

I GOT TO THE FIELD EARLY WITH THE JCB AS I wanted to have the job finished by nightfall. John Patrick Murphy had recently returned from England and had bought this field from Jim Dowd. It was very uneven, being overlaid with mounds and boulders and enveloped in an ample growth of whins. Evidently it had been in that condition for many a long day; I had an Ordnance Survey map at home, drawn in 1837, and it showed all the mounds and scrub just as they still were. John Patrick intended to clear the field and make it a profitable investment, so he asked me to level it. I told him my price and the bargain was made.

It was by no means a big job, so I reckoned six hours would see it complete. In one corner there was a circular mound which looked like a small rath. If I had been superstitious I would have been reluctant to disturb the fairies underneath, but I wasn't; I had bulldozed several of them before, without retaliation. There was one small problem, however: in the middle of the little rath there was a boulder which was too big to be moved by the JCB, but I had arranged to get some gelignite to blow it apart. The agent, who was to carry out the job, was due around dinnertime.

I started to work on the side nearest the road, digging away the mounds, filling in the ditches and leveling the ground. It was easy work, and very pleasant on a summer's morning. The field was on top of the hill of Knockaculleen, so I had a tremendous view out over the sea past Aughris Head where the island of Innishmurray was squatting in a blue haze - that was a sign of good weather. From beyond the brow of Ballykillcash I could hear the hum of a tractor mowing a meadow. Men passed by on their bicycles, whistling as they pedaled their way towards the bog (they wouldn't get past the village, if I knew some of them).

Around eleven o'clock John Patrick came across the field with a tin can in one hand and a string shopping bag in the other. He hailed me and I knocked off the engine.

'I have a drop of tea here, Pat.'

'And it's welcome too,' said I, 'I was just beginning to feel thirsty.'

We sat on the grass leaning our backs against the wall. John Patrick opened the bag, took out two mugs, and set them on the ground. Then he unrolled the sandwiches that his wife had neatly packed and handed one to me. He took the lid off the tin can and poured two mugs of tea.

It was while we were eating that we saw Tim Foley coming through the open gap. He was very old, thin, slightly stooped, and he walked with the aid of an ash plant. Slowly he made his way over the uneven ground and with difficulty he sat down on a stone beside us.

'That's a fine day, Tim', said John Patrick.

'Tis indeed,' replied Tim, 'thanks be to God.'

'How are they all down in Dromore West?'

'They're all well indeed.'

Tim took out his pipe, tapped it a few times on the base of his thumb, searched in his pocket and produced a piece of plug tobacco, which he proceeded to pare with his pen-knife. Having filled his pipe he struck a series of matches until he finally had the pipe glowing. Puffing away, he pushed back his head and looked about.

'I heard that you were working on the field, so I came up to see it before you had it flattened. It was a grand field. I remember playing here when I was a gasur - no bigger than the stone I'm sitting on. You know, it was a great place for rabbits. Every mound and ditch used to be riddled with rabbit burrows. It was great sport to come up here with a ferret and a hound. You'd catch dozens of them - enough to feed a family for a week.'

'They made a nice dinner, sure enough,' agreed John Patrick, 'but they were a curse all the same. You couldn't put down a crop or they'd cut it to bits. I think myself that it was a good idea to get rid of them.'

'I don't know about that,' countered Tim. 'Many a big family was reared on rabbits - what they didn't eat they sold - and they would have been in a bad way if the rabbits weren't there. I wouldn't mind so much if they went out and hunted them down for food; but to bring in a disease to destroy them, ah, that was a crime.'

'It was the only way, Tim. They would never have got rid of them otherwise.'

'Ah, no, it was a crime; it was a crime,' mumbled Tim as he sucked and puffed at his pipe.

'Well, rabbits, or no rabbits, we have to get this field leveled,' said John Patrick, getting up and stretching himself. I got up as well, flexing the stiffness out of my limbs.

'Thanks for the tea, and tell the good woman that her sandwiches were delicious.'

'Don't mention it,' replied John Patrick.

As we were moving away Tim raised his pipe in his right hand: 'Tell me. Are you going to level the rath in the far corner?'

'Of course we are,' answered John Patrick. 'It's all good land and I can't afford to waste any.'

'You shouldn't go near the rath,' said Tim seriously. 'It's been there since the beginning of time and it will bring bad luck on the man who interferes with it.'

'Come on now. You're not going to start telling us about the fairies,' joked John Patrick, and turning to me he asked, 'do you believe in fairies, Pat?'

I laughed. 'Well, I've bulldozed a few raths before and they haven't hit back at me yet, so I'll chance another one.'

Again we were about to depart when Tim halted us. 'What about the stone that's in the middle of the rath?' he asked.

'That's a bit big for the digger,' I replied, 'but I have a man coming around dinnertime to blow it up.'

Old Tim shook with emotion and stood up on his unsteady legs. 'You're not going to blow up that stone!' he wheezed in astonishment.

'Why not?' I asked. 'It's in the way, isn't it?'

'That's no ordinary stone,' hissed Tim. 'That's called the Bleeding Stone.'

'Well, the bleedin' stone is destroying the corner of my field and it has to go,' said John Patrick making deliberate use of the vernacular.

'Do you know the legend attached to that stone?' asked Tim, becoming more passionate.

'No,' answered John Patrick. 'And what's more I didn't know there was any legend attached to it.'

'There you are,' said Tim in a tone of mingled irony and triumph. 'You're destroying something and you don't know the value of it. That stone and the story behind it are greater than me and you because we last only one lifetime but they have lasted hundreds of lifetimes.'

'What is the story?' said I, going back to lean against the wall.

'We can't be wasting time listening to the raveling of an old man,' John Patrick declared impatiently.

'There's no hurry, I'll get the job finished before night.'

'There was a lord in this locality one time,' began Tim, adopting the detached tone of the story-teller, 'whose name was Mac Giolla Cais. He was extremely wealthy and had the finest fort in Tireragh, the remains of which you can see to this day beyond in Carrownrush. Mac Giolla Cais had a beautiful daughter called Aoife and it was said of her that she was as dear to the poorest peasant in the quarter as she was to her father.

Once, a poor travelling poet, Art O'Connor, arrived at the fort seeking the Lord's patronage. Mac Giolla Cais, a generous patron of learning, thought that the young poet had promise and gave him an honored place among his household.

When Art saw Aoife he immediately fell deeply in love with her and began to compose the most wonderful lyrics in her praise. At the next feast, when he was summoned by the lord to recite some of his verses, Art chanted those he had written for Aoife. She herself was present and was moved by the sensitive passion of the lyrics so that she, in turn, fell in love with Art, but without realising that the poems were addressed to her.

For many months Art continued to write poems expressing his love and every time he recited them Aoife was his most attentive listener. He never betrayed that it was to her they were dedicated, for he believed that such a beautiful, such a noble maiden would have little regard for the affections of a poor poet.

As for Aoife, she assumed that Art had a mistress somewhere who was the subject of his poems. Her youthful mind brooded on the hopelessness of her love and she lost interest in food and companionship.

MacGiolla Cais grew anxious about his daughter's well-being and summoned the doctors and druids. But none could tell him what her ailment was.

When she was very weak she asked the servants to carry her to the banquet room so that she could hear the poet. On her arrival Art chanted a new poem he had written expressing his sorrow at his mistress's illness. Aoife, not realising that the poem was for her, thought only of Art's mistress who, in her illness, had such tender lyrics to comfort her. Her heart broke between love and despair, and she died, falling at the foot of the dais on which the poet was standing.

All the people of Tireragh were heartbroken at the death of Aoife; so beloved was she that thousands gathered at the fort of Mac Giolla Cais to sympathise with him and to attend her burial. The young men went out beyond the fort to a green spot and dug her grave; around the grave they threw a high mound so that mankind should not forget where she was buried. No sooner was her body laid and covered than a mysterious thorn bush sprang from the spot, budded and flowered in an instant.

Art, in the mean time, was grief-stricken by the death of Aoife. He was requested by Mac Giolla Cais to compose an elegy for the funeral, but he was so paralysed by grief that he could not, and he vowed he would never again write a verse.

When the funeral was over and the people had dispersed, Art went to the place where Aoife was buried. He threw himself prostrate on the grave. His sorrow was so great that he was unable to utter a single syllable, but he determined to stay there until death should release him to follow his beloved.

Three days and three nights he lay there. On the third night a wind blew from the west and the leaves and the boughs of the thorn bush began to flutter and whisper. As the wind grew stronger the whispering became louder until it was audible and articulate. It was the voice of Aoife telling of her hopeless love for the young poet, Art.

The realisation that Aoife had died for love of him swept over Art as the sea in storm sweeps over a curragh. His horror pressed like a murderous ocean on his soul. And yet death denied him its mercy. But Aengus, son of the Good God, who was always sensitive to the anguish of the lover, became aware of Art's plight. In a twinkling he came. Taking pity on Art, Aengus touched him with his hazel rod and turned him into a rock.

That same rock has rested upon the grave of Aoife from that day to this. It is said that if anyone tries to move it from its beloved spot, the rock will bleed. That is why it became known as the Bleeding Stone.'

Old Tim paused when he had finished the story. His eyes had a distant look; but the distance into which he was looking was not outside him: it was somewhere deep within. He took his pipe from his mouth and examined it; it had quenched for lack of attention while Tim was involved in his story. Striking a match he asked: 'You wouldn't move that stone, would you?'

John Patrick turned angrily to me: 'For Christ's sake, will you get to work and stop wasting time listening to shit like that. If that frigging rock is there for a couple of thousand years it's bloody well time someone shifted it.'

I got up on the JCB and started digging again. Old Tim was watching me closely. I felt sorry for him in a way; every time the bucket sliced into the earth it seemed as if it was cutting into his own flesh. Old lads like him were very attached to the land; no wonder, I suppose, when they had stories like that to tell about every stone and every tree.

I was working (under the close scrutiny of Old Tim) for about half-an-hour when a van halted at the gate. It was the agent with the gelignite. He took a case from the back of the van and came to us across the field.

'Hello Pat. Where's this rock?' he asked me.

'It's over here,' John Patrick shouted abruptly.

The two of us followed John Patrick. I glanced behind to see Tim's reaction. I had to smile. The way he was sitting erectly with his eyes open and alert he reminded me of a rabbit in that perplexed moment of terror after it sights danger and is deciding whether to stand or flee. Then he got up and followed us at a distance.

The agent surveyed the rock, looking all around it, standing back to assess its size and, finally, poking at its base. On one side of it grew the thorn bush that Old Tim was talking about. I wondered if there was anything to his story, if the rock really covered a grave.

'It will be easy enough to blow this,' reported the agent. 'A couple of sticks at the base should crack it open.'

He opened his case and took out two sticks of gelignite and a coil of fuse. He put the two sticks in tightly under the base of the rock; then attached the fuse and unrolled the coil.

'We'll take shelter behind that mound over there,' he said to us, and shouted to Tim: 'You had better get down well behind that mound, sir; there will be bits of rock whistling past your ears in a minute.'

John Patrick and myself got in behind the mound and called on Tim to do likewise. Presently the agent lit the fuse and came up to join us.

'Come on, old man, you have sixty seconds to get down,' said he to Tim.

Old Tim stirred himself but, to our amazement, instead of ducking behind the mound he made for the rock.

'Jesus, what's he doing?' cried the agent.

I got up to run after him; but John Patrick grabbed me by the jacket. 'For Christ's sake, do you want to get killed too?' he roared.

I looked over the mound. Tim was approaching the rock and the fuse was still sizzling. He reached the rock and I saw him fumble about at the base. He took out the sticks of gelignite, held them in his hand and turned to walk away with them. At that I ducked my head into the earth and covered my ears with my hands. But I heard it, nevertheless, a dull BOOM. I was afraid to raise my head and when I did I was confronted by two faces that mirrored my own feelings: they were white with fear and dumb with disbelief.

I will not describe the scene that lay before us when we approached the rock. It is sufficient to say that poor Old Tim was blown to bits and the rock, the Bleeding Stone, undamaged, was drenched in blood and gore.

Even yet, and it is now years since the incident, I have not resolved the question that it posed to me. I have pondered it endlessly, turning it over in my mind, trying to analyse it, but I have never succeeded in breaking it down to rational terms; hence I have never reached a rational conclusion. I suppose that is the real nature of a mystery.

I need not add that the Bleeding Stone is still there. Nobody has tried to move it since and I doubt if anybody ever will.

Baptism of Water

8.30 A.M. THE CARS JERKED AND JOSTLED slowly and ill-humouredly along Main Street. Down the deserted footpath Mr Joseph Cavanagh strode morosely past the shop fronts, their gaudiness faded by the morning light. Mr Cavanagh thought of them as aging whores: their painted attractions might be tolerable in an indulgent darkness but were repulsive in the merciless clarity of the dawn. This analogy occurred to him every morning since he first thought of it ten or twenty years earlier.

At the corner of William Street he had to step off the kerb to make way for three men staggering towards him evidently senseless from intoxication. Two of them were trying to carry their companion, his arms slung across their shoulders, their faces tightened in an expression of gigantic determination. He was rocking from side to side muttering drunkenly, "We'll die flying, like Daly's hen." Mr Cavanagh paused to let them pass.

His habitual journey to school led him off Main Street and down the hill to the river. He never paused on this journey which took exactly twenty-seven minutes. But on the first Tuesday of every month the cattle auctions in the town mart blocked the riverfront with cars and trucks and trailers. Accordingly on the first Tuesday of every month Mr Cavanagh was delayed on his journey and was late for school.

When he had picked his steps fastidiously over the green film of cowdung which covered the ground he stopped on the bridge, rested his briefcase on the parapet, and examined his shoes to ascertain whether he had preserved the immaculate shine his landlady had so conscientiously imparted to them the night before.

To his chagrin he found the toes smeared and even the tips

of his trouser-legs stained with the green slime. He took a tissue from his pocket and tried to purge himself of the odious filth, but without success. Mr Cavanagh was deeply vexed. Not only would he be late for school that morning and have to face Moroney at the interview debilitated by feelings of guilt but his confidence would be further undermined by an impaired self-image caused by the stain and stink of cowdung.

The Headmaster had summoned Mr Cavanagh to come to his office at ten o'clock that morning. The subject of this tête-à-tête was not communicated but Mr Cavanagh knew that, however it might be camouflaged with trivialities, the important topic was the lack-lustre performance of his students in the public examinations.

Moroney would scratch his sleek head and comment on the success of the school football-team and inquire how rehearsals for the school opera were progressing, but sooner or later he would open a gambit with a throw-away comment such as, "I see your boys didn't do you justice in the Leaving." And without accusation or condemnation he would proceed to deliver a homily on the importance of examination results and the precedence of English - "a key subject" or "a core subject," depending on which cliche was in vogue with him.

Mr Cavanagh gave up trying to restore the shine to his shoes and tossed the tissue over the parapet into the river. He watched it being borne swiftly away by a current which was pulsing with vigour from the early autumn rains.

Moroney would, no doubt, drop a few references to Finnegan, the President of the Board of Trustees, who was "keenly interested in the welfare of the students." Mr Cavanagh almost smiled. If Finnegan were anxious it would only be in fear that he might somehow lose votes for the next County Council election. A local shopkeeper, he posed as a "man of culture", "a lover of the arts"; but his love of culture found no higher expression than the purchase and consumption of a bottle of French wine with his Sunday dinner.

Thoughts of Moroney and Finnegan made Mr Cavanagh weary, so weary he could have stretched himself out on the ground.

> *I could lie down like a tired child,*
> *And weep away the life of care*
> *Which I have borne, and yet must bear,*
> *Till death like sleep might steal on me.*

The words of Shelley, which he had ground into generations of students, came into his mind. What irony that Shelley should be the grist for Moroney's mill, Finnegan's mill, yes, and Cavanagh's mill - he could not deny the reality; he was no more than a drudge. In his own lifetime Shelley was hounded to death by their likes, just as he would be hounded to death now - an anarchist, a bigamist, an enemy of society. How nauseating that they should smile on him now and utter complimentary platitudes, they who would shrink in horror from what Shelley was advocating if they believed that anyone would take him seriously.

Mr Cavanagh thought of a good comment for Moroney, one which he nevertheless knew he would not deliver: 'If I taught Shelley properly, Mr Moroney, the boys would burn down the school instead of passing their Leaving Certificate.'

He looked at his watch. Already he was ten minutes late. The thought of turning back occurred to him, declaring himself sick for the day. But no, that would be too cowardly. Why should he flinch before a pigeon-souled creature like Moroney?

Then he did an extraordinary thing. Standing on the bridge, resting against the parapet, he lit a cigarette. Mr Cavanagh had never before paused on the bridge, not to mention loitering to smoke a cigarette. He inhaled the smoke stiffly but deeply and gazed down the river where it opened into a lough.

Shelley probably made his absolute protest by drowning himself in the Italian sea. But his was the despair of the full man who could not persuade his people to share his vision. The despair of the empty man was different.

Mr Cavanagh looked into the river and found it indeed seductive. It would be soothing to fill the void within him, even if it were only with water. It would be at least meaningful to die like Shelley in one final fierce gesture; in Mr Cavanagh's case it would be the only gesture he had ever made. It would convulse the mean world of Moroney and Finnegan; it would shake the youth out of their bland indifference; nothing would be the same, could be the same, afterwards. Or would it?

Perhaps his death would affect only one life - his own. Moroney would be annoyed at having to look for a new English teacher. The students would inquire if they were getting a day off as a result of the tragic event. The ripples on the water would fade away, and the accustomed state of tranquil torpor would be quickly restored.

Beneath the arches of the bridge the waters were gushing through, divided but not tamed by the abutments. Where the waters joined again they created little dancing whirlpools, angry little maws on the surface of the river. Round and round they spun, down and down, turning and sinking, ever converging upon their internal infinite.

Mr Cavanagh saw as the greatest obstacle to suicide the loss of decorum involved in clambering over the parapet of the bridge, jumping fully-clothed into the river and perhaps, worst of all, shouting for help once he found himself in the water. And he imagined himself doing just that, regretting his decisiveness, struggling with the water, grasping after a shred of meaningless life, battling passionately to preserve an entity called Mr Joseph Cavanagh. Yet it would probably be obvious, even then, even in that predicament, that Mr Joseph Cavanagh had already died. Even if he reached the bank it would be a new Joseph Cavanagh that would pull himself out of the water. Washed away would be the old man stunted by years of mediocrity, dead the disgruntled teacher, drowned the aging bachelor. And the new man born of water and impetuous action would go, dripping wet, to Moroney's interview and tell the little fat man that Shelley didn't write poetry so that boys could pass the Leaving Certificate or shopkeepers make polite conversation, but so that men could be free of their imaginary shackles. Then, reaching out, he would pluck one of his jowls by way of resigning.

Mr Cavanagh was feverishly excited by this train of thought. The possibility of new life far outweighed the risk of getting drowned. Yet the first obstacle was still insurmountable.

After a moment of perplexed thought a calm descended on

his agitated mind. He glanced around furtively and when he was certain that no one was observing him he took up his briefcase and flung it into the river. With mischievous delight he watched the brown leather bag float rapidly downstream. He imagined the copy-books within getting water-logged, the ink running over the pages and from one page to the next, making incomprehensible essays illegible, until 'A Day at the Seaside' was united with 'The Countryside in Winter' in one mass of sodden pulp.

When the bag finally disappeared into the distant lough Mr Cavanagh looked at his watch. He would be just in time for his interview with Moroney. With the smug satisfaction of one who has just purchased a coveted object at a fraction of its normal price, he resumed his journey to school.

Gelding

YOU ASKED ME WHETHER SEXUALITY IS A bridge or a barrier between man and woman. I don't know the answer. Who can say? Who can be dogmatic about anything in this life?

But your question resurrected a strange memory of an old experience, raised it like a ghost from a long-since landscaped cemetery; and, like a Lazarus summoned from his slumber, it has been haunting me ever since, loitering aimlessly at my shoulder, waiting perhaps for an explanation as to why it had been disturbed, perhaps even waiting for some gesture of dismissal.

I had an affair many years ago with a girl called Deirdre. It was one of those sultry affairs, passionate but full of unease and uncertainty. One evening I was waiting for Deirdre in a coffee shop on the North Circular Road just a few streets from the Psychiatric Hospital where she worked. It was the same place in which we usually met. In fact our evenings together were entirely predictable, in an unpredictable sort of way; it was as if we were acting out a drama for which the scenario had been written already, yet each performance, being live, generated its own tensions and its own suspense - hence that feeling of uncertainty I mentioned. As a man of the world, you will understand exactly what I mean. You too have often been racked by the same dilemma: Will she? Won't she? At my place? At hers? In the end she always did, but not until I was stretched to a fibre with expectancy. And yet she wasn't the tantalising type, definitely not that type. I think her uncertainty may have been the result of an inward struggle against the voluptuousness of her own nature. The struggle was pointless, as she always came to realise, eventually, thankfully.

But this particular evening was to be different, very different. I waited for her in that deserted cafe, sitting among formica tables under garish Italian tourist-posters, breathing-in the steamy odour of pasta, planning my seduction strategy, indulging in lustful thoughts.

When she arrived I was immediately struck by the seriousness of her expression: her face was slightly drawn, her eyes meditative. It was disconcerting. Her habitual mood was one of gaiety and joy; she was almost profligate in the diffusion of her emotional warmth. Furthermore, her mood was buoyant; never before had I seen that bright face of hers totally submerged in the gloom of the moment. What could be the matter?

She sat down at my table, opposite me, and ordered a coffee from the waiter who had ambled over after her.

'Hello,' I greeted her probingly.

'Hello,' she responded with the momentary flash of a smile evocative of a faint sunburst through a bank of dark cloud.

'Did you have a difficult day?'

'It was dreadful.'

I knew that she was working in the ward where they kept the most disturbed patients. She never talked about her work, but I had often suspected that she found some of her experiences harrowing.

'Where would you like to go? I have tickets for the cinema, the International, but if you're not in the humour we need not go. We can go to a disco instead.'

'No, the cinema is fine. Which film?'

'Onibaba.'

'Oney what?'

' "Onibaba." It's Japanese. I think it means "The Hole".'

'Not another one of those,' she replied with mock-weariness in her voice, yet again with the slight hint of a smile. She was referring, of course, to a current penchant of mine for Japanese films. There had been a stream of them flowing into the city in those days - it was the heyday of Shindo, and Shinoda, and Kurosawa - and I never permitted one to drift away again without having seen it. So the unfortunate Deirdre (or Mary, or Ann, for that matter) was dragged along to witness Samurai massacres, and battles, and harakiris. The only relieving factor was that she often missed gory scenes because she was preoccupied trying to keep abreast of the sub-titles.

Nevertheless, I was anxious about bringing Deirdre to see that film on that particular night, because of her evidently low spirits. She was insistent that we go, however, and there was absolutely no putting her off.

You are quite familiar with the film, so you will understand immediately that it was not the best choice of entertainment for a girl whose nerves were raw. I was surprised that she survived those early scenes where the Samurai warriors fall to their death down the hole that the two women had so cunningly contrived as a trap. Oddly, it was at that comical but bizarre scene where Toshiro Mifune runs through the long grass almost crazed by his sexual frustration, that she first began to flinch. And while Mifune rolled and roared in frenzy, poor Deirdre grabbed my arm and buried her forehead in my shoulder. I sensed something of the depths of her nausea, the gush suppressed behind clenched teeth. Taking her hand as gently as I could, I led her out of the cinema.

She did not want to go to a restaurant or a bar, so I brought her back to my flat. There I put a match to the fire I had readymade in the grate and opened a bottle of Spanish wine.

Soothed by the soft firelight and the sweet wine, Deirdre began to recover. We sat on the carpet, close to one another, our backs resting against the side of an armchair. In hesitating phrases and long intervals of silence she started to explain what had upset her.

Working in her ward of disturbed patients that morning, she had gone with another nurse to carry out a routine check on a patient in one of the padded cells. He was prone to violent fits, but his aggression was never directed against other people, so they had no worries about entering his cell. When Deirdre peeped through the door she found him lying quietly in his bed. She entered the room casually with her colleague, and they began their inspection. Immediately, something caught Deirdre's eye. It was a blotch of red blood seeping upwards through the white sheet that covered the patient. For a moment she was shocked. She glanced at the man's face. He was staring at the ceiling, engrossed, as if he were unaware of their presence. And on his face, Deirdre said, there was the strangest expression she had ever seen, an expression of total serenity, utter calm, absolute peace. She quickly snapped back the sheet. What she beheld she described in monosyllables, holding her face in the palms of her hands in an effort to repress the nausea that kept welling-up inside her, threatening to spill over at any moment. The man's groin and stomach were a mass of blood and raw flesh. His hands too were bloody. At first glance it looked like widespread self-mutilation. But when she examined him closely, it became clear what had happened: the man had castrated himself with his bare hands; with his fingernails he had torn out his own testicles. Can you imagine? Deirdre told me that she saw wads of flesh-tissue still lodged under his nails.

Was it any wonder that the poor girl had recoiled from the image of Mifune ranting and raving frenziedly in the long grass? I was shocked on hearing her account of the incident; how much more shocking it must have been for her who had experienced it.

Deirdre slept in my arms that night, but any thought of sexuality between us would have been unconscionable. Never before had I seen the girl so defenceless, so vulnerable, so passive. In that, possibly, lay the reason why I did not wish to press home an advantage. Or maybe I had lost all appetite for sex after listening to her account of that gruesome incident. I was certainly unmanned by it. Lying there, wide awake, with Deirdre's soft body close to me, I could not wrench my mind off the lunatic who had castrated himself with his bare hands. One detail of Deirdre's description had particularly fascinated me, the unearthly expression of peace on the man's face. It had even puzzled Deirdre. Did he feel that a lifetime of torment was over? Or was there any coherent thought in his mind? That calm, that serenity was exasperating, as if, somewhere far beyond the frontiers of rational thought, he had driven a salient into the bulwarks of ultimate wisdom. It vexed me deeply, because, even though I could not understand his state of mind, a bothersome intuition kept insinuating that his was the condition of every man, that, if there was a difference between the torture that had driven this lunatic to pluck out his testicles and the torture of any ordinary man suffering the anguish of hopeless love for a woman, it was a difference of degree and not of kind. That same lunatic might have been burning with a passion for the girl next door, or for a secretary at his office, or even for one of his nurses. What if he had been in love with Deirdre?

I looked at her sleeping innocently in the crook of my arm. Never did I feel so close to her before. This closeness was partly, if not totally, due to the abandonment of sexuality. Of that I am certain. That presence, which had chaperoned my relationship with her up until then, which by turns had acted as buffer and plaything and go-between, was for the first time absent, banished by a madman lying mutilated in the lunatic asylum, and I found myself alone with my girl for the very first time; united in the sympathy and innocence of that moment, she was to me a sister more than a lover.

On that night I fell in love with Deirdre, and never met her again.

That is the experience. I tell it to you as precisely as I can recall it, and I leave you to draw your own conclusions, if you are so inclined. But beware - they were very special circumstances and it might be dangerous to make a generalisation based on them.

Queen B

MONDAY WAS HIS NAME, BECAUSE Monday was his day. Monday was a B, a very disgruntled worker B. Drudging and monotonous his life, his future appeared equally dreary and unpromising.

Sunday night in the grey and cheerless dormitory, Monday was now top of the queue. He was in the first bunk, and the other five were occupied by worker Bs in chronological order down to the far end where the spry figure of veteran Saturday hardly sagged the final bunk. Sunday, of course, fat voluptuary, was not there; it was his night in the chamber of the Queen B.

For Monday the craving had been building up from the middle of the week and was now at its most intense. Waking or asleep he had no escape: racked between repulsion and attraction, he dreamt of delectable disgusting honey of generation oozing in dewy beads among black hairs on soft flesh. Spurred by his fierce desire he would rise at dawn the following day and labour unceasingly in his allotment, gathering the succulent stems of the wild scutch grass and the petals of the crimson poppies. At sunset he would take up his bundle and carry it to the chamber of the Queen B. As usual, she would mutter and grumble while she rummaged and nibbled, with never a pleasant word of gratitude and never a compliment.

But when she was sated with food she would lie back on her couch and slowly raise her arm to expose - o heaven, o hell - her armpit, his personal armpit, with black hairs on soft flesh, and o, the bitter-sweet syrup of oblivion beckoning to him in beads of crystalline sweetness. And he would creep up, for how could he resist! And with his tongue he would lap the fullness of her secretion, suck the luscious loathsome honey of generation, assuager of all torments, balm of all sores, sedative of all anxious thoughts. For the whole night he would lie oblivious in the bed of that armpit, all pain, all depression suspended, until the first cold trickle of grey reality filtered into the chamber. Then the arm of the Queen B would be lowered, like a surly portcullis, and the armpit, his armpit, folded away for another week. With no more ceremony than when he arrived, and with less display of emotion, he would depart.

The days of the week were seven, because the armpits of the Queen B were seven; and the number of weeks in the month was four because every fourth week the Queen B laid her clutch of eggs.

Sitting on the edge of his bunk, using several of his long black arms in the exercise, Monday aimlessly rotated a metal disk which he had found in his allotment. He was brooding, as he frequently was, on the emptiness of his existence, the pointlessness of his drudgery, and the relentless craving which enslaved him to his treadmill. Every week he thought of leaving. But, just as often, he failed to overcome his dependence on that one night of oblivion; just as often he flinched at the prospect of a future without the occasional obliteration of consciousness. Once, he tried to rebel against the indignity of his situation by refusing to go to the chamber of the Queen B on his appointed night. Defiant, resolute, he lay in his bunk. The other workers surrounded him and begged him not to upset the blessed pattern of domestic order. Monday was unmoved. They threatened to break one of his arms, so that he would no longer be able to maintain his position in the Queen's household, but would be dragged to the frontiers of the domain and flung over the boundary wall to fend for himself among the hungry nomad Bs in the wilderness beyond. He was not daunted. Then Thursday, the most reflective of the seven workers, explained that if Monday refused to go that night, then Tuesday would have to become Monday. That was enough to convince him. Life was bad enough. His grasp on time and place was feeble enough without losing whatever semblance of identity he already possessed. He could not suffer the humiliation of having to become Tuesday or Wednesday. He yielded. Picking up his ignominious bundle he proceeded to the Queen's chamber and entered with apologies and excuses for his unpunctuality.

The weeks and months rolled by, as nature had ordained. Every month a new batch of eggs was laid, fertilised by the white dust of procreation falling from the whisker of the worker as he lapped the honey of generation. Ceremoniously the eggs were borne to the boundary wall of the domain, and there dumped unceremoniously into the wilderness to perish or survive as chance should determine. And the whole cycle seemed to Monday as pointless as it was interminable.

Slowly and decisively, Monday stopped rotating the metal disk. Using a sharp corner of the bunk-frame, he scratched the word NO into its polished surface. He then scooped out a hole in the ground, buried the disk, and covered it over. With the same deliberate motion he passed down through the dormitory for the last time and out the exit door. Outside he paused for a moment and glanced around and up at the great dome of the heavens. What a wide place the world was, now that he experienced the freedom to explore it!

North, south, east, or west,
Which direction will I find best?

He picked the east, fixed his eye upon a hill afar off in that direction, and hurried towards it as quickly as his skelter of legs could carry him.

As he approached the boundary wall he was conscious of an array of beady eyes glinting in the wilderness, peering at him, observing his course, hungry eyes that would scour the seven allotments of the domain in the first light of dawn to confirm his going. And then the ritual of challenge and combat would be initiated to determine who would take his place; he who succeeded in killing or maiming all his rivals would step into the domain before evening to claim his prize.

Monday would have liked to stay and watch the contest; he would even have liked to loiter long enough to see the warrior emasculated by that same prize. But he dared not. The craving was too strong. He had to keep moving, to put as wide a buffer as he could between himself and the object of his craving.

And as he passed through the night he heard the buzz of

conversation from the encampments of the nomads, and the sweet whistle of the ilka-bird. He jogged to the rhythm of the brooks, and somersaulted in delight at the sight of a tumbling star.

By the time daylight came, Monday was far away from the domain, among new hills and strange meadows. He felt that he had now distanced himself sufficiently from the location of his former way-of-life to have broken its hold. Down in the grass he lay and slept lightly and happily for a long long while.

When he woke up, the crisp yellow sun was high in the heavens; a warm breeze redolent of shrubs and flowers came rolling over the plain; and the timber boughs of the treetops reverberated the music of birdsong. Truly this was a new birth, in unimagined and unimaginable contrast to his former existence.

Down the meadow, Monday saw the most beautiful sight he had ever seen, a princess B passing over the earth with a grace that left him breathless. He hurried down to observe her from a closer vantage point. In her path the buttercups bowed their heads in deference to her more exquisite loveliness. She was at that most beautiful time of life, fully grown, on the verge of maturity, soon to be a queen, yet retaining all the vernal innocence of youth.

Monday was following her, automatically, unconsciously, when she stopped, turned around, and faced him. It was an embarrassing moment for Monday, who stopped dead and stared at her. But she smiled at him, and radiated a beam of such warm vibrations that his embarrassment melted away; the limits of his isolation quite dissolved, and the darkest corner of his spirit was illuminated. He responded out of the growing fullness of his warmth and light, transmitted similar rays through the prisms of his shining eyes, until either soul basked in the other's radiance. And the most wonderful thing of all, to Monday, was the fact that this absolute mutual understanding, this profound emotional exchange, happened instantaneously, unadulterated by the profanity of sound or touch.

She turned, as if in total confidence that the ecstasy would last. He followed. Their movement was a joyful dance, like the bucking of the first lamb of spring, full of the newness of the world, full of the wonder of experience freshly felt.

And for a month, Monday gladly followed the graceful movements of the princess B. Loth was he to take his eyes off her, even for the fraction of a moment; nothing could entice him from her presence, even for the fraction of a fraction of a moment. In brief intervals of reflection, Monday realised that he had been completely shrived of all his lustful cravings. Indeed he had almost forgotten his life with the Queen B, until a raw and jealous wind blowing from the bitter north whispered in his ear that the Princess herself would soon be a queen. The image of his beloved Princess transformed into an ugly bloated female horrified poor Monday. Out of his despair he cried aloud to the trees:

> *O, how shall I*
> *stop*
> *the trickle*
> *of the sands*
> *of time? How?*
> *O, how shall I protect my darling*
> *from the fate-rot*
> *of ripeness? How? O, how?*

And the oak, the oldest and the wisest of the trees, answered him in a low and measured monotone. He told Monday that there was one antidote to the fate-rot of ripeness: the Princess would have to eat the berries of the magic rowan that grew on top of the highest peak of the mountain; she would have to eat the fruit of the tree of imagination.

Monday was so relieved, so overjoyed, that he tumbled in somersaults across the meadows. The Princess followed him, smiling indulgently at his display of excessive delight. Then he led her directly to the slopes of the mountain, and they began the long climb towards the highest peak.

Long they dallied on the lower slopes and frolicked among the blossoms of the purple heather. Long they dawdled with the mountain rabbits and sprawled in unconcern upon the banks of quickly moving streams. Then, beset by anxious thoughts, they would strive for a long while and move further and further up the mountain slopes.

They reached the base of the highest peak. The sun was shining, the sky was blue, and the air was clear. They lay down to admire the great spread of the landscape stretched out before them. Not a puff of wind was blowing to cool away the heat of their endeavours. The Princess reclined with her graceful black arms behind her on the rising ground. Monday was below her, gazing fondly up at her.

It was then that he noticed it. Horror of all horrors! Too late they were, too late in reaching the tree of imagination. The process of maturation had begun; the rot had already started to take its course. Glistening in the sunlight that shone down on her exposed armpits, Monday beheld honey-beads swelling to succulent ripeness, heaven and hell materialising before his eyes. Transfixed, powerless, he shuddered with pain and ecstasy. His lustful hunger, like a river that had been building up behind a dam, fell upon him with a hundred times its original force.

He did what he had to do. He crept up to her, embraced her, and with his tongue in her delicious armpit he lapped the honey of generation, opium of workers, syrup of dreams.

For seven days and seven nights they lay embraced at the foot of the peak, Monday devouring the first fruits of the Princess's abundant harvest. From one armpit to the other he went, tasting bliss in the soft fold of each, until finally the week was spent.

After the seventh day the Princess arose and stood a little way off. She was changed. Now she was a queen. For a little while she remained motionless and self-absorbed, as if she were trying to come to terms with the metamorphosis. When she eventually began to move she did so without any reference to Monday; without turning towards him, she began the journey down the mountain. He followed, a little way behind, no longer equal - dependent, addicted, manacled.

When they reached the level ground the Queen did not stop; she continued on, commencing the quest for a suitable domain. Far and wide she ranged. Monday took no part in the search; he merely followed where she led. The Queen had now assumed absolute responsibility, her self-importance swelling like the eggs in her ovary, and Monday was reduced to the status of an appendage.

At length they came to a domain which, from all appearances, had only recently been vacated; the structures of the buildings were still intact and the seven allotments still neatly divided. The death of its former queen was the probable explanation why it had been forsaken and yet left in such an excellent state of repair. The Queen took possession of the quarters appropriate to her, and Monday retired to the dormitory of the workers.

Already there was a massing at the boundary and a contest imminent to decide who should occupy the other six positions.

Monday found the dormitory to be cheerless and grey, exactly like the previous one he had known; the bunks here too were laid out in a neat file, six of them. He went up slowly to the first bunk and sat down on it. Drained by despair, he felt a sense of the utter impossibility of freedom. His eyes bent on the beaten clay of the floor. In front of him he noticed a little patch where the clay was looser than anywhere else. Impelled by a vague recollection, he quickly dug into that patch, his many hands working through the soft clay with impetuous speed. Presently he struck, what he suspected he might find, a shining metal disk. Taking it up and rubbing off the dirt he was able to read the letters scraped boldly on to its surface, 'NO'.

Three for Oblivion

THEY WERE THE ODDEST GROUP I EVER picked up since I started working the Lethe crossing. Three of them there were, so separate yet so similar, so wrapped up in the rags of their self-importance. They were loitering on the pier - where I picked you up just now - holding their backs towards one another, trying to pretend that their journeys would never overlap, that their destinations could not possibly coincide. I may as well admit that I do not understand your fellow-countrymen; but I find them amusing, and intriguing. Yes indeed, they never cease to intrigue me.

The charred remains of their clothing were ripped and shredded, rendering the three men indistinguishable one from another were it not for the spectacular exception of their ties. Whatever catastrophe had sent them here together had evidently been powerless to bleach the colour from those strange pennants which hung loosely, noose-like, about their necks.

When I pulled the boat up to the pier they boarded so silently, so sullenly, so formally, you'd think they were in the regular unpleasant habit of catching the ferry. Sullen as they were, I was glad of the business, for business does not often come my way. Indeed what could be more futile than the occupation of the Ferryman on Lethe? Old Charon, up on Styx, has a fine time by comparison. He gets the full stream of traffic entering the Underworld, and he gets it first. By the time he relieves them of their coins there is nothing left for the rest of us - as if Styx were the only river they might want to cross. But I believe that even Charon is complaining lately. They come as penniless as paupers, expecting to be ferried over for nothing - you'd think it was a social service we were running instead of a business. O yes, and I've heard that some of these fly-boys are pulling the wool over poor old Charon's eyes, cutting the shiny buttons off their habits and passing them off as coins. And you've seen Charon: you know how old and doddery and blind he is; he can't keep up with all the changes in currencies and thinks the buttons are minted by some of these new countries that send us so much business nowadays. But don't get me wrong - I'm not sorry for the old bag: he has his fortune made and should have retired long ago. It's the attitude to authority I deplore. No respect. They have absolutely no respect for authority.

As bad as things are for Charon, they're far worse for me here on Lethe. Those who journey this far do not come to catch the ferry. They bathe in the river, and take the waters; occasionally they swim across. I suppose you could describe this as the spa of the Underworld; although, if you want my opinion, that treacle-black slurry is far less inviting than a sulphur bath. But it has its qualities, I'll admit, and its cure is guaranteed! They come from all over, you know - the ones that want to forget, the ones that are burdened with guilt, the ones with the dark secrets - and look, see how thirstily they swarm around the waters. I must tell you a phrase, coined by a former passenger, to describe that scene; a very disdainful gentleman, but generous, very generous, he was viewing the scene from that same seat in which you are now sitting; he turned scornfully to me and said, 'wouldn't they remind you of flies around a shite.' An excellent analogy, don't you think?

Now you realise what a ridiculous job I have, providing a ferry service on Lethe, waiting for the occasional passenger to make his way on to the pier. You can also imagine how happy I was to pick up the three Irishmen together, even though one glance suggested that they carried not so much as a can of paint for the sodden timbers of my old craft.

I pushed off from the pier and rowed out into the stream, bearing an open mind as to the course I should take with my passengers. You will understand that, if they had naught to pay their passage, I was perfectly entitled to dump them overboard and let them swim to shore minus their precious memories. On the other hand, I should mention that I am very liberal as to the form of payment. I am prepared to accept any trifle. Indeed, I regard even an interesting conversation or a humorous anecdote as a tolerable reward for my labours. Those alone I abominate who make no offer whatsoever, either by way of goods or by way of conversation.

When I reached midstream I eased up on the oars and let the boat drift idly with the current, just like this. For a while they paid no heed; they were probably trying to convince themselves that the situation was normal. Eventually the silence grew tense and shuffling, until it was broken by an outburst from the one I shall call Green Tie, for want of any other method of identification.

'Hey, mister, is this your coffee break or something? Why don't you lean on those pins? I can't stay floating around on this bleedin' pond forever, you know.'

'We shall resume our journey as soon as you meet your obligations,' I replied.

'What do you mean?' he snarled defensively.

'You haven't yet offered to pay your fare,' said I.

'Look, mister, if that's your idea of a joke, then I'm laughing, laughing like hell - HA -HA -HA - sorry if I don't sound amused. Now you can get on with the job like a good man.'

'I am not joking. You have taken the ferry; you must pay your fare. Surely that is not an unreasonable request.'

'You know damned well that I have no money to pay fares.'

'Then you shouldn't have taken the ferry,' said I, lifting the oars out of the rowlocks. 'But I am in no hurry, I can wait until the three of you decide to pay your way, if you should wish to proceed farther.'

'This is ridiculous,' took up White Tie. 'I thought that, coming down here, I would at least have no more worries about transport strikes.'

'I lived in a high-rise block in Belfast,' stated Orange Tie, 'and I always had a dread of getting caught in the lift between floors. It never happened to me in Belfast; I had to come down here to get caught. It proves a lot of people wrong: Belfast is not worse than hell!'

Each and every remark was addressed directly at me, yet the realisation that they had been surprised into talking in each other's presence embarrassed them, and they fell silent once more. At length it was Green Tie whose restlessness got the better of him.

'Listen, mister. I'm giving you one last chance to get those oars moving. If you don't take that chance now, I'm going to relieve you of the oars. And you could get injured in the process.'

'Let me relieve you of any illusion you may have that you can resort to violence,' I replied calmly. 'Let me remind you of my somewhat superior station here. I may not be numbered with the gods but I do share something of their calibre.'

That took some of the wind from Green Tie. He sat back on the seat and stared sulkily out the starboard side. Another long interval of silence followed.

'If you won't row us over,' faltered White Tie, 'perhaps you wouldn't mind bringing us back to the jetty.'

'Cast your eyes towards either shore,' said I, 'and you will observe that it is as far to travel back as to travel forward. You may choose the shore of your destination, but either way you must pay the toll.'

'But I have nothing to offer you in payment,' wailed White Tie in desperation. 'So what option is open to me?'

'Why the obvious one, of course: you can swim to either shore.' I enjoyed watching the expression of horror that welled up into their three faces simultaneously.

'Not bleedin' likely,' declared Green Tie belligerently. 'And have every last thought flushed out of my brain. Not bleedin' likely.'

'The reason I took the ferry was to keep my memory intact,' said Orange Tie.

'What is so important about your particular memory?' I asked. 'Everyone else is driven by an anxious desire for amnesia. The waters of Lethe are regarded as the great consolation of the Underworld; why do you shun them as if they were poison?'

'Where I come from,' said Orange Tie in an intense but reflective tone,' memory is sacred. It is as sacred to us as the tablets of stone were to the Jews. Do you understand? And the images engraved on our memory are just as durable as anything that was written on those same tablets. We remember what happened at the Boyne and on the walls of Derry. Those deeds are an example, a guide, a standard, a point of reference around which we mould our lives. Memory is the great storehouse of our tradition; it gives us identity and individuality; we would be nothing if our minds were not well fortified with memories of what our fathers and forefathers stood for and fought for.'

'What a restriction on your life your memory must have been,' I exclaimed. 'You should have tried to escape from it. You should have sought freedom; it would have been a higher aspiration.'

'Ach, no, that's nonsense. If it weren't for memory and tradition, what would mark me off from any Fenian; what would make me different from the Provo get whose bomb sent me here?'

Green Tie shifted uneasily, aggressively.

'Memory is a wonderful thing,' sighed White Tie, anticipating a conflict between the other two. 'If it hadn't been for my childhood memories of the West of Ireland, I should have found life in the city unbearable. And I am sure that I could not now face the prospect of eternity without the succour of those same cherished memories.'

'I have discussed this subject with countless people on board this boat,' said I, 'and only one of them appeared to me to have a sensible reason for clinging to memory. He was a cynical rascal of a gentleman, but very generous. He maintained that his amorous exploits in the Upperworld were too good to be forgotten, and he was going to try and smuggle his memories of them into Elysium. I wouldn't have given much for his chances, although, on the other hand, I wouldn't be surprised if he succeeded; he was a resourceful scoundrel and had a way with people.'

'What do you think of our chances of getting into Elysium?' asked White Tie.

'I think there is very little possibility of that. People nowadays have such misconceptions, it never ceases to amaze me. They think that, if they have done nothing wrong, they have lived a good life and, so, should qualify for admission to Elysium. It isn't like that at all. On being born into the Upperworld a person is endowed with a potentiality for living. It is up to him to realise this potentiality, to live life fully and deeply, and thereby to develop his capacity for life. Without a highly developed capacity for life, a person is in an alien element when he gets to Elysium, like a fish in the air, like a swallow at the bottom of the sea. There is a severe need for a prophet to go to the Upperworld and explain these things to them. Since the days of the Empire, people have gone very badly astray.'

'Do you mean the British Empire?' interjected Orange Tie hopefully.

'There was only one empire worthy of the name, the Roman Empire.' Orange Tie wilted in the glare of disgust that I could not help directing at him. 'None of you appears to me to have developed any capacity for living. For dying - yes. Your whole nation has developed an enormous capacity for death - as if death conferred value on anything. The sign of death is stamped on every frustrated impulse, every guilt-ridden joy, every achievement envy-maimed. You worship death with an idolatry far more fervent than that of any Dionysiac. You come to us with disease in your eyes, with decay in your hearts, with death in your stillborn souls; and you have the arrogance to think that you are well-qualified for eternal life. No, my friends, you will not be admitted to Elysium. If you are not consumed in your effrontery by the wrath of Jove, consider yourselves lucky. When you set foot on the Elysian shores you will, no doubt, be directed for re-cycling: all residue of conscious thought will be expunged from your minds and you will be sent back to the Upperworld with the opportunity of fulfilling at least some of the potentialities with which you will be endowed.'

'That doesn't sound so bad, but do they use any discretion as to where they send a person?' inquired Green Tie. 'Surely they would send a person back among his own people.'

'Where a person goes is a matter of absolute chance.'

'You mean that, if I go back, I might be born into a Loyalist house, and grow up a bleedin' Orangeman, ignorant as to who I really am.' Green Tie sounded extremely worried.

'You might end up in the most unlikely place indeed. But how can you be so sure as to who you really are? You may have twenty lives over you already among different races and religions. So why should you regard your last one as more important than another?'

'I don't care what you say,' roared Green Tie. 'I'd rather rot down here than risk going back up there as a Protestant. I have some patriotism left in me yet.'

'And I'm going to take no chance of going back as a Fenian and a Papist.' Orange Tie jumped to his feet and spat the words into the face of his fellow-passenger.

'Maybe we should turn around then and go back to the jetty.' White Tie got to his feet as well and stood between them to prevent a brawl. 'We don't have to go to Elysium; millions before us have been content to remain in the teeming caverns of Hades. There, at least, we will have the comfort of our memories. For my part, I have no desire to be born again. If I were going back to the Upperworld, I would like to remember; I would like to see my children and my friends; I would like to visit the places I have loved. Otherwise, I see no purpose in going back.'

'What an enigma you are, the three of you: you find it so hard to live together; yet, you managed to die together. How did you contrive that?' I asked.

'We must have been caught in the same bomb-blast in Dublin.' replied White Tie.

'In Dublin!' gasped Green Tie. 'I must have forgotten. The fumes of this bleedin' river must be affecting me already. If it was in Dublin, then it must have been a Loyalist bomb.' He turned viciously on Orange Tie. 'I suppose it was your bomb, you licker of Britain's arse-hole.'

'Bugger-off, Napper Tandy. I'm proud to say that I have defended the Union, and I did whatever I was called on to do. But, to the best of my recollection, I was in Belfast when the bomb went off.'

'Come to think of it, I might have been in Belfast too. Yes, I was to go there on business. It's very hazy.' White Tie was racking his muddled brain - so much for his valued memory.

'I bet you were in Belfast,' exulted Orange Tie. 'And we know who was likely to be letting off bombs there. Don't we?' He advanced menacingly on Green Tie. 'You Provo bastard, I'll bet it was you who pulled the gaff on the three of us.'

'Let there be no violence here,' shouted White Tie. 'It's this eternal hostility between the two of you that has put us in this predicament.'

'You keep out of this, you lush slob. You're probably a Provo sympathiser anyway.'

'I certainly am not a Provo sympathiser, and I have never condoned violence and murder. All civilised Irishmen believe that murder is a greater evil than any political arrangement of which they may disapprove. I include myself in that number and reject the use of violence as a means towards any end.'

'Oh really?' inquired Green Tie. 'Tell me this then: did you pay taxes when you were in your cushy job back in Dublin?'

'Of course I did.'

'And those taxes were used to pay and equip an army. And that army was told to support the institutions of the state - by violent means if necessary. Look, brother, you believe in violence just like the rest of us, so don't be such a bleedin' hypocrite.'

'That's different,' cried White Tie indignantly.

'There's only one difference,' roared Green Tie. 'You hire your gunmen; I carry the gun myself.'

'You were carrying the bomb that killed us, weren't you?' interjected Orange Tie. 'Admit it, you bastard.'

'I don't remember,' retorted Green Tie, squaring up to him, 'but I don't give a bleedin' curse whether I was or not.'

Genuinely worried that a fracas might overturn my boat, I

roared at them, 'Sit down, the three of you, or you'll all end up in the river.' I handed my drinking cup to White Tie. 'Take a drink. It will cool you off.' He took the cup and looked at it, hesitating.

'Go on,' I said. 'It will do you a lot of good, and a single drink has no lasting effect on the memory.'

He leaned over the gunwale and scooped a cupful of water impetuously from the river. But when he looked at the contents of the cup he was perceptibly shocked. For a few moments he continued staring into the cup. Then he smelt it, and tasted it.

'I don't believe it,' he gasped. 'It's stout, porter, a whole river of it.' He turned his blank uncomprehending gaze out on the black expanse of Lethe.

The other two looked over his shoulder. Orange Tie took the cup, smelt it and tasted it. 'It's bleedin' Guinness all right.'

'A riverful of draught stout? I always knew that I'd go to heaven,' cried Green Tie in ecstasy as he in turn took a sample from the cup. 'It's stout alright, but it's not Guinness, probably the stuff they brew in Cork. Murphy, that's what it is.'

'Well, where does this river rise? In which brewery?' Orange Tie addressed me light-heartedly, as he took another sample from the cup. 'It's no wonder they're swarming around the banks.' He scooped another cupful from the river. 'Not a bad head on it either. Look.' He pointed to the yellow froth he had managed to generate by the impetus of his hand.

The three of them sat back in the boat, passing the cup from one to another, admiring the froth, tasting the water - which they maintained was stout - comparing it to the brew served in taverns back in the Upperworld. Politics, religious divisions, violence, all such considerations faded quickly in the light of this new-found common interest. Around and around went the cup. They imbibed drink after drink. Presently, I knew they must be reaching the stage where the waters take their ordained effect, but I said nothing. Why should I try to stop them? After all, they were far more amenable, far more content. The change was undeniably for the better. There they were in the back of the boat, arms around one another, united as they had never been united before, attempting to sing:

And we'll all go together
To pluck wild mountain thyme...

Singing became progressively more difficult as the last residues of memorised data were expunged from their minds. Finally, unable to recall any more words, they fell inarticulate, and just continued humming and rocking to-and-fro to the rhythm they had already established.

I must confess that I was tempted by a cruel thought. To return and discharge them in their senseless, oblivious state on the pier where I had picked them up. Did they deserve any better? Come, be honest and frank; would it have been such an outrage to withdraw them from circulation? I think no-one would have condemned such an action; many might have applauded it. As usually happens, however, my generosity got the better of me. I addressed them as follows. I might as well have been talking to myself, of course, because they were now incapable of understanding a single word I said.

'Gentlemen, it is now of little moment whether you immerse yourselves in Lethe or not. But, since I undertook to ferry you across, I will complete the task. When you arrive on the Elysian shores you will be dispatched forthwith into a new life, and I hope you make more of your opportunities the next time around. Now, I always insist on payment, as a matter of principle; the only objects you appear to have that hold any interest to me are your ties; they have some colour, so I may be able to use them to decorate my boat. I will take your ties in payment of your fare. Agreed?'

They offered no objection, so I relieved them of their ties.

As I resumed rowing towards Elysium, they appeared to me the most pathetic of sights, huddled in the back seat, arms still entwined around one another. Without their ties they were now totally indistinguishable, and I could no longer recall who was who. Which of them was Green Tie, which Orange Tie? I had no way of making out. But what did it matter? I suspect they were far more similar to begin with than they would have been honest enough to admit.

I hung the three ties together from a pole on the stern. Have a look. Don't you think they look decorative? Green, white and orange. A curious combination of colours - but they do brighten up the drab outline of the boat.

You may have noticed that we have been drifting in midstream for quite a while now. I hate having to be blunt with people - it is not my style at all. But, since we left the pier, I have been hinting at it in the broadest possible manner: you have been sitting there without opening your mouth, without offering any token in payment of your fare.

BIRDS

A Message to Sparta

DON'T BE FRIGHTENED. I MEAN YOU NO harm. Honestly! Please forgive this rude interruption. Where were you going? To lunch? Back to work? I really am sorry for delaying you, but it is necessary, and I shall not detain you long.

I need you. I need a witness, and a messenger. Then we shall both be free, and you can return to your chores.

I do apologise about the gun. But try to pass no heed. There is one round left in the chamber, and it is not for you. So please be patient. All I ask of you is your indulgence, and a little of your time.

You are still staring at the gun. I quite understand, believe me. I too hate guns. I hate them passionately. What ugly little snouts they have! The gun must be the most depraved invention of mankind, don't you think? In a world full of green and living things, this obscene device exists for the sole purpose of snuffing out life. Have you ever thought about it? A simple little tool that fits snugly in the grip of your hand, as might a saw or a hammer - pull a lever, and wham, a lump of metal is sent tearing through someone's skull, shattering bone, tearing sinew and nerve, mushing the grey brain inside. The victim keels over, someone whom someone called father, or son, someone that was capable of love and laughter, now reduced to a lump of rotting meat.

But please excuse me. I must not indulge my morbid obsessions. You are obviously in a hurry and I did not detain you for a discussion of guns.

This is my room. Days on end, weeks on end, I sat here contemplating the deed I must now perform, fondling this repulsive piece of metal, mustering the will-power to bring my life's work to its inevitable conclusion. But the more I thought about it, the more futile my proposed action appeared, the more futile indeed my whole life appeared, unless I left behind some testimony, unless I sent back my own dispatch from the front, my personal message to Sparta. And that was my purpose in hijacking you.

You do not seem to have recognised me yet. A few years back you would have recognised me immediately. I had a moment of public attention. I was celebrated as the battle hero from the Valley of the Cuckoo. Now you recall! That illustrious battle in which everyone perished except one! The advancing column of our Militia met one man emerging from the battlefield, and declared a glorious victory - for our side.

Yes, that was I. And this is the same gun I was carrying. There were six rounds left in the chamber then. Now there is one. I swore that day over the dead bodies of my family and friends that I would use each round to eliminate a carbuncle of hatred from the backside of the earth. And so I have, so I have.

Commanders all! One after the other! It took time, but it was easy for a war hero. No one suspected. The security meetings credited the enemy with each assassination, and were baffled by the ease with which they had infiltrated and struck. The fools, the fools!

Yes, there is one round left, enough to eliminate the biggest festering carbuncle of them all. It is frightening how hatred can grow within our very souls, like some fungus multiplying in the dark when we are least aware of it, until the light of dawn reveals how it has spread its venomous spores into every corner of our being.

It was my father's gun, this Luger. I picked it from his hand on the battlefield. What a ludicrous weapon with which to go to war! And what an unlikely warrior carried it into battle! A man so gentle I had seen him side-step rather than bring his boot down upon a slug!

It was probably manufactured before the Great War. Like

many other weapons in our village, it had been stashed away for generations, until the morning of the Battle. Eight rounds the Luger takes, and only two of them were used. I wonder what my father did with those. Ludicrous for a military engagement it may be, but it is perfect for an intimate assassination.

Enough of such things for the moment. Let me tell you about the Valley of the Cuckoo. To us the name was apt. Never did the bird find a more melodious berth than it did in the scrub of that valley floor; nowhere did the cuckoo arrive so early in the spring, nor linger so long into the late summer. And while it was forsaking all its other haunts the cuckoo returned faithfully year after year to our valley.

I was born there. I grew up there. Everybody I knew, everybody I loved was living there. You have an idea where it is, tucked away in the Western Mountains. When I was growing up it was the most peaceful corner of the earth, despite being in the so-called front line of a so-called civil war.

We hardly realised it was in the front line until that day the Commander of the Militia so informed us. We hardly realised there was a war going on down through the years. We were not totally oblivious to events, of course, and we had our guns tucked away. But until the day of the illustrious Battle I had never heard a shot being fired in anger .

Was it laziness, or cowardice? The Commander of the Militia thought it was both, that day he arrived in his little jeep and observed that we were living in relative harmony with our neighbours across the valley.

Hardly a mile separated our two villages. A stream flowing through the bottom of the valley was the dividing line between their territory and our territory. Crossing the stream was a makeshift footbridge. Whenever that footbridge fell into disrepair - and it was constantly required for the returning of strayed sheep and goats - it was fixed surreptitiously in the dead of night by men from one side or the other. That was one of the conventions of our peace: men did not enter the bottom of the valley during daylight for fear of offering provocation. Hence the heavy growth of grass and weeds and scrub! Only goats and sheep could extract sustenance from those neglected acres, and only women and children could be seen to herd them. Once in a while a frisky buck from either side would discharge a shotgun into the air to enjoy the sight of a clutch of young women scuttling for cover back to their village. Such actions fell within the conventions as well and were never taken seriously.

All changed that day the Commander arrived. He was a man from another world. He looked so powerful, so aggressive, so fearless in his combats, jumping out of his jeep, barking orders. But I lived to see him cringe like a beaten mongrel. I saw him with abject terror in his coward's eyes. I saw him kneel and beg for mercy. But not a morsel had I left.

I am horrified to confess that I took immense pleasure from killing him. When you hate somebody as intensely as I hated him, when you have him totally within your power, when you have a gun in your fist, and pent-up behind that fist is a whole reservoir of emotion, then the release which comes with the pulling of the trigger is overwhelming. Even when he slumped at my feet I felt nothing but exultation. I even kicked him into a ditch with the toe of my boot before I departed.

He looked more formidable that morning he arrived in our village to inspect the local Militia. Militia! Men were embarrassed and puzzled, trying to remember what the word meant, what the purpose of it was, what responsibility they had been neglecting. It was like that. The village had simply forgotten about the war.

But by mid-day the confusion had been dispelled; the official members of the Militia had been mustered and assembled in the village hall. They looked farcical, those middle-aged men, in their bits of creased uniform, with their motley collection of small arms. The younger men and the boys had never been inducted into the Militia. My friend, Johnny, and I happened to be there because we were festooning the hall in preparation for Johnny's sister's wedding later that evening. We overheard the address of the Commander, the haranguing he gave the local Captain whom he blamed for the state of disorder. He was quite a rabble-rouser, that same Commander. He knew how to pluck the strings of guilt, how to fan the grey embers of forgotten fires. He was surprised, he said, that our village was prepared to settle for a fraction of what was ours by right. The whole countryside had been ours until we had been jostled out by the intruders, who left behind their progeny to be nourished by our land for the rest of time, and our shame had been perpetuated in the very label that was attached to the valley afterwards, the Valley of the Cuckoo. That was an arrow to the heart sure enough! We had long revelled in the lyrical title of our valley, had prided ourselves on its association with birdsong and summer. To have such cherished images so suddenly shattered, so ruthlessly daubed with excrement in our minds, was a shock indeed.

The Commander also declared that the opposing village was the simplest target imaginable for mortar fire, that a single heavy gun and a dozen shells would be enough to blast it from the side of the hill. He would leave the following day and return as soon as possible with artillery and reinforcements.

Johnny and I looked at each other, stunned by the proposal to blast the village across the valley.

Let me explain what that village meant to us. Since my childhood I had been looking across at it without hostility and without fear. Indeed I regarded it with awe, imagining a privileged life-style, houses exotic and luxurious, opulence throughout. This image was the fabrication of a child's mind, but it was shared by all children, and, as there was so little communication across the divide, the same image survived unchallenged into adult perceptions.

It was easy to be in awe of the other village. The white walls of its houses were picked out and lit up by the morning sun. And whenever mist erased the rest of the hillside, those brilliant white gables seemed to perch in mid-air, floating in front of us like some mystical representation of the New Jerusalem. What I discovered eventually, what Johnny and I discovered, was that the villagers on the other side regarded us in exactly the same way, except that it was the evening sun which cast an aura around our village, with our white walls haunting them through the long twilights. Isn't that ironic?

How, therefore, could we be expected to blast this icon out of the sky? We found the idea abhorrent. But it was worse than that for Johnny and me. We had lately been visiting the village of our supposed enemies. We had made friends there.

We quietly withdrew from the hall and went out the back to confer. We were particularly worried about Buttons. He was the gifted accordion player whose reputation had lured us across the valley in the first place. Johnny was a singer and had an insatiable appetite for music and new songs. When he had mastered all our own songs and had heard all of our own tunes a hundred times, nothing would do him but to explore what the other side had to offer. And, of course, he persuaded me to go with him.

It was difficult at the beginning. They didn't trust us. But when they heard Johnny singing to the accompaniment of Buttons, and when they saw the immediate warm bond that was forged between them, they stopped suspecting and made us welcome.

Buttons was blind. He had two white discs for eyes, and I don't know whether they or his skill on the accordion gave him his nickname. He was also an old man by the time we met him, and he had a thousand tunes and the words of a thousand songs. He could sing, but not well, so he enjoyed enormously teaching Johnny his songs and then accompanying him on the accordion to the delight of everyone who cared to listen.

And people listened. Every night that we stole over to their village became an occasion of music and song and celebration. They enjoyed our songs as well; in many cases the airs were similar to theirs and the words only somewhat different.

During those first visits we could not help noticing how similar their village was to our own, how the people were no richer and no poorer, but just as generous and warm-hearted, how the girls were just as beautiful but even more alluring because they were unattainable.

After a while, Johnny decided it would be good for our village to have Buttons over for a session. I was anxious, but no argument would dissuade Johnny. He was right of course. The two of them made a huge impression, and after that there was no party, or family celebration, or public function, to which the two of them were not invited.

Of course Buttons was due to attend the wedding celebrations for Johnny's sister. We were worried. With all this stirring of hostility, we wondered if it was safe to have Buttons over. We also wondered whether we should alert the other side to what was happening. In the end we decided that we should not allow this little khaki terrier to deflect us. We were hopeful that he would go away and that the village would very quickly and very willingly forget his visit.

Buttons came that evening and played as he had never played before, because it was Johnny's sister's wedding. Johnny sang, but I had often heard him sing better. In fact the whole occasion was shadowed by the consciousness of a dark threat.

When the music ceased, and the greetings had developed into farewells, Johnny and I took Buttons back down to the path and set him of his way, as we had done dozens of times before. Once he was on the path he had no difficulty tapping his way back to his own village.

But he never made it. The next morning our village was astir with the news that Buttons had been found shot dead on the footbridge. Two women out driving goats to pasture had discovered him lying face downwards on the bridge with a bullet in his back.

We were certain, Johnny and I, that it had been the Commander. But he was no longer in the village, when we enquired; he was gone to get the reinforcements. We pledged then with white-faced teeth-grinding determination that we would make him pay.

Eventually I did make him pay, all he could pay at least. For if he had died a thousand times, and squirmed in the muck a thousand times begging for mercy, he could not compensate for the destruction of our village, could not repay the cost of a single gentle life from either village in that forgotten Valley of the Cuckoo. He died like the dog he was, kneeling before me, whimpering. But I thought of Buttons and Johnny, and the dozens of other lives he had destroyed, and without hesitation I put a bullet straight through the centre of his forehead.

I got so much satisfaction from that killing that I knocked off the other four in exactly the same way. And they all died like dogs. But they were buried with full military honours, big funerals, speeches, salutes, talk of heroism. All the while I wanted to shout from the rooftops: no, they were not heroes but snivelling cowards, and they were not the target of enemy assassins, but were dispatched by me, me, your battle hero from the Valley of the Cuckoo, wreaking vengeance for the deaths of your enemies and of my kith and kin.

All through the day Buttons lay on the bridge, no one daring to approach him. By evening Johnny could tolerate the anguish no longer. He felt responsible for Buttons's death, and couldn't stand the thought of him lying alone with no one to attend to him. I helped him locate a handcart, but when we reached the top of the path he insisted on proceeding alone. In full view of what must have been an array of watching eyes across both sides of the valley, he pushed the cart down the path to the footbridge. It took him some time to manoeuvre the body up onto the cart. Then he pushed forward up the hill to the white-walled houses on the opposing brow.

The following morning the handcart was left back on the bridge with Johnny's dead body sprawled across it.

That put the cap of death on the whole valley. There was motivation now, and anger, and lust for revenge. A general mobilisation was ordered by the Captain. This time there was no laggard response. Even the young men and boys who had never been inducted into the Militia turned up and were handed weapons with cursory instructions in how to use them.

I refused to join. When they were all finally lined up for the impending battle, the Captain summoned me. He reminded me of my obligations to my people and to Johnny who had been my friend.

I told him it was because of Johnny and Buttons that I would not fight. I told him the Commander had shot Buttons deliberately to put us at the throats of our neighbours. I told him to wait and shoot the Commander when he came back; then there would be some point to his mobilisation. I turned away and began to walk out of the village. He ordered me to come back or he would have to shoot me. I told him to go ahead, that it made as much sense as shooting the people across the valley.

He didn't shoot, as I knew he wouldn't.

I had climbed well across the brow of the hillside by the time I heard the first rounds being fired. I lay down on the barren hilltop petrified by terror. I tried to make my mind blank so that I could not imagine what was happening below. To and fro across the valley the sounds of battle rolled, sometimes so intense I could not distinguish individual shots in the concentration of continuous gunfire; sometimes it lulled to occasional sniper fire. To compound the terror I could smell burning and see billows of black smoke rising into the sky over the valley. What were they doing to each other?

When night fell the gunfire ceased altogether. I was expecting renewed outbursts at dawn, but dawn arrived in a shroud of morbid silence. There were no more sounds from the valley.

I could try to describe the scene of devastation and slaughter which spread out in front of me as I returned down the hill, and you would probably be shocked, and you would probably be moved; yet no description could convey the horror with which I observed that panorama of wanton carnage. Imagine your own home, the locality where you live; imagine the dead and mutilated bodies of your father, mother, brother, sister, of all your relatives and friends strewn about that landscape. Think of some lovely little family of babies and toddlers that you know; now imagine them all burnt alive with their mother inside their home. Imagine a similar family that you don't know; you come across them burnt alive in their house; and you have to say to yourself: my brother, my cousin, my friends did this.

No more. I am sick at heart. I can think no further on it. Not a single living thing could I find in the whole valley.

Dazed, I walked up the eastern road. I had one thought on my mind, to find, and kill the Commander, who was responsible for this devastation of my home. When I met the approaching column of the Militia, I scoured the faces, hoping to blast him on the spot. But I could not locate him. My immediate elevation to war hero served my purpose and I coldly bided my time.

My soul's delight is that I have eliminated five Commanders. But my soul's dejection is that I have achieved nothing, for no sooner was each of them struck down, than a new one sprang up in his place, younger, stronger, more rabid than the first. And worse, far worse affliction for my tortured soul: every time I look into a mirror now I see the image of another commander; I see the cold hard eyes manifesting the hatred underneath; I see the obsession with killing, the rejection of life.

With one round left in my father's Luger I shall exterminate this final commander, and feel that at last I have eliminated one who will not be replaced.

Now, you are free to go. You are free to do what you will. Of course I will be in your debt forever if you convey to the people my small experience of this glorious war .

PAINTER

I F YOU HAVE COME, GREY-EYED TRAVELLER, ON a journey to our remote town, then the likelihood is that you have come to view the work of Somerville, the painter. You will find it, most of it, exhibited in our luxurious Heritage Museum. You will also wish to visit his house and studio, carefully preserved as they were at the time of his unfortunate death twenty years ago. No doubt, you too have been mystified and attracted by the romance surrounding his last picture. Why else would you bother to journey so far? But you will not be disappointed. The guide will point it out to you on your tour of the Museum, not casually - the way she will point out the other works arranged carefully to demonstrate all the phases in the development of his short but spectacular career. No, no, these are all but the prelude to his final piece, 'Figures in a Wood', which will be the climax of your tour. It is housed in appropriate isolation in a bay strategically located before the coffee bar and the souvenir shop. The guide may be young, but she is well trained; she knows that all that has gone before is merely an elaborate appetiser, that this is the main course, and that she must serve it with panache before she dismisses you to the antechamber for coffee and souvenirs. And if you are listening carefully to her commentary on the painting, instead of admiring her sloe-black eyes and the tantalising flick of her head with which she clears her eyes of her fall of hair, you will hear her begin with the words, "And now ..."

She will tell of Somerville's last months when he is reputed to have locked himself away from the world to work on this, his masterpiece, how he strove manically for perfection, how, in despair of achieving such perfection, he attempted to destroy the painting and killed himself with the same knife (which she will indicate - lurking in its own glass case in a corner of the same bay). She will point out the slash mark on the painting, and the tiny splashes of the painter's blood preserved faithfully beneath a thick coating of varnish. As you will notice, there is no guile in this lovely daughter of our town, and she is totally unconscious of irony when she ends her commentary with the words, 'Of course with modern restoration techniques, the Museum could have repaired and restored the painting to its original state. It was decided, however, to preserve it in its damaged condition, since it is the knife-mark and the blood that people come to see.'

You will not feel mocked. Nobody does. And you will take a closer look at the picture, as she will invite you to do. But what do you see, dear traveller? What does your eye, grey from staring at all those long roads, tell you about that simple composition? Look closely at the painting for a moment instead of at the guide. She will wait. It is all planned, and you are allowed these few moments for quiet personal contemplation.

So, what do you see? Three figures! Trees! A two dimensional composition! Greens, browns! Come, look closer, the figures are not so abstract. You can discern more if you look closer. Start with the trees. Somerville always did - start with the background, that is. Doesn't it strike you as ironic that a painter living in urban squalor should use such a bucolic setting? The large tree on the right-hand side of the painting shows Somerville's attachment to geometric shapes. If you let your eye run along the spreading root, up the trunk, along the spreading branch, it will describe a perfect circle, the circumference of which runs through the centre-point of the rectangular canvas. You are not overwhelmed by this observation? Yet it was that circle that killed Somerville!

I assure you I am not mocking you. Look at his next additions. The male figure reclining under the tree is part of the circle and reinforces it. The female figure in the centre of the picture completes it. Look at that figure. What a lovely pose: the graceful swing of the torso, the angle of the neck and head as she glances over her left shoulder at the youth! How powerfully this figure completes that circular movement! What a bond is established between the girl, the boy, and the natural background!

Somerville never used models. People shunned him. There were no offers from voluntary sitters. Anyone who saw his work would not have been tempted to pose out of vanity. He scarcely had the money to pay for his materials; to pay for a model was out of the question. When he visited the shop to buy his meagre ration of groceries, the loveliest girl in the town recoiled from his presence. When he walked down the street at the shop's closing-time, he was always disappointed when she crossed to the other side of the road, depriving him of a closer look at her sloe-black eyes and full lips.

And so he painted from his imagination, figures that were suggestive, situations that he had experienced in pain.

Look at the figure on the left-hand side of the painting. It is large, obviously to balance the mass of the tree. But how keenly can your grey eye see? Can you observe, for example, that this dejected hoary figure is a self-portrait, the only self-portrait Somerville ever attempted? Can you see also that the choice of arrangement and the tone of this figure follows a whole sequence of failed attempts to break that circular bond between the girl, the boy, and the natural background. These other attempts are all there, covered over in layer upon layer of paint, there to be seen if you would only concentrate the intensity of your vision on the picture instead of casting glances at the ripe breasts of your young guide.

Somerville brought you to our little town, but then our little town brought Somerville to you and to the world. At the time of his death he had sold scarcely a dozen paintings. His life's work was already conveniently collected, stored within the confines of the little terraced house which will be the next stop on your itinerary. Our far-seeing Mayor bought the lot, paintings, house, everything, for the municipal authority. They came cheap. Nobody wanted the house after the tragedy, and nobody wanted the paintings because the critics and the commentators had not yet discovered their worth. It was also our Mayor who had the Heritage Museum built to exhibit the paintings; it was he who had the house restored for showing to travellers; it was he who lured the critics back with lavish banquets to have another look, to discover for themselves that Somerville was a genius; it is he, our Mayor, whose statue is in the middle of the town square.

Once he had painted the tree, the boy, and the girl, he left them and did not tamper with them whatsoever. They were complete. On the other side, however, all was in a state of flux. Even the underlying geometric design that Somerville relied on so much kept changing. In his first version of the self-portrait he attempted to extend to it the treatment and tone of the other figures; the result was an idealised figure of an older man curved towards the centre, towards the girl, with a suggestion of profound longing in that concave arch, in the expression on the face. However, as a composition it didn't work. This new figure failed to relate to the others. The arc it formed went off into space; nothing within the picture held it in control or completed its circular course.

Short of interfering with the figures themselves, he tried every stratagem to weaken the bond between the girl, the boy, and the tree, to set up a pattern of relationships that would extend to this new figure. He introduced minor shapes, a branch of the tree, a dash of foliage, a small animal in the undergrowth. But all failed. He returned, therefore, to the self-portrait and re-cast it, this time in a vertical frontal pose, no longer idealised, but meditative, detached. This was a failure too: in picking up the mass of the tree-trunk, it over-emphasised the vertical shapes, destroying the rhythm of the movement he had already established. It was almost as if the twist of the girl's torso was mocking him.

The final attempt, dear traveller, you can certainly see. The knife-slash from the top to the bottom of the figure you may find distracting, but close your eye to a slit and you will see it entire as Somerville painted it. This time he got the composition right. Arched away from the girl, from the boy, from the tree, the figure sets up an opposing circle and curls into a pose of rejection. What is it rejecting? The girl? Youth? Nature? Why does Somerville, in this instance, portray himself as being older, uglier, even more dishevelled than he was in reality? Was he finally seeing himself as others saw him, a filthy ragged tramp who lived in worse squalor than the least of his fellow townspeople? Was it the pile of canvasses that were increasingly more difficult to preserve undamaged in the cluttered interior of his house that was oppressing him? Or was it the girl with the fall of dark hair and the sloe-black eyes, she whom he captured in essence in this painting, captured in the lovely curve of her shoulder, in the sensuous line of her ripe breasts?

Your time is up, dear traveller; another drove of your kind is massing at the entrance. The final summons from the guide allows a brief moment for your foolish questions. No, of course she never met Somerville - he died before she was born; but her mother remembers selling him groceries, although she doesn't recall ever having spoken to him.

That is it. Cast one more glance at the famous painting. You are at a distance now and can see not the figures, nor the wood, nor the knife-mark, but your own reflection looking sheepishly back at you from the glass. Take a good look at the lovely pointing fingers of the guide before you retire to your coffee and your souvenirs and the endless grey roads awaiting you.

Bonds

FROM THE DARK INTERIOR OF THE GASCOYNE, Fonsie Glennon watched the pavement drying. He had just scoured the strip beneath the tables, and out further, out to where the pavement dropped over the high kerb. Boulevard Adolphe Max. Always busy. People passing. Coming down from Place Rogier and the Gare du Nord, or up from the shopping complexes around De Broukere. All going somewhere. All tip-toeing over the wet pavement to get to their destinations.

Water mat wearing to patches, disappearing rapidly in the heat of the afternoon sun. Fonsie pulled his cigarettes from the pocket of his apron. Lit up. No customers in the afternoon. Brief lull. He enjoyed the relief of resting his bulk. Not so good later when the customers returned, when he would have to hoist himself out of the chair and return to serving. However.

Block across the way boarded up. Ugly. Defaced. Scabby with torn posters. The whole district was scabby. Every second block being pulled down. Mass concrete and glass going up. The Gascoyne too would disappear in rubble. And he would regret it. Yes. Not for the job. He would get another, probably with better pay. But he would miss the way-of-life. Old-fashioned. Lazy. Undemanding.

The radio caught his attention. Humming away unnoticed all day. Music station. Flemish. It was he who always tuned it to the Flemish station. Hated the French, the Francophones, their arrogance. Didn't have Flemish, needless to say. Just the few words. Enough to get by. Hardly listened anyway. But now. A Greek tune. Plucking strings of memory. Strained his ear to make out the comment at the end of the record. Something twenty years ago. Of course, 1974. The fall of the Colonels.

Twenty years. Could it really be? Another Greek tune. That instrument? The bouzouki.

Yes, the bouzouki. That lifted Fonsie Glennon back twenty years all right. Out of the banal occupation of his barman-waiter routine. Back over the years of genteel exile in the European capital. The rearing of two children. The continual shunting to and fro between Belgium and Ireland, summer and Christmas. Back over the tedium of his married life. Back to when he opened a thousand doors. A thousand doors. Only to watch them swinging idly in the wind, only to watch them one by one blow shut again. Yes, the bouzouki brought him back.

It had been a pilgrimage, his pilgrimage. Strange one for a Roman Catholic clerical student. To Delphi. Mount Parnassos.

He told her about it. They often sat together in the coffee shop after lectures during that last year of their degree course. Not the same lectures. She had done French and German, he Theology. But someone had introduced them, and they would sit down at the same table if they spotted one another. He had found her attractive. Yes. But then he was a clerical student and that was that. She had such a casual attitude to everything. Very different from his own. They talked easily. A kind of banter. Even about serious things. He told her of his dream of going to Delphi. Not just Greece. Not Athens. Delphi.

She teased him. Delphi? His vocation. Was he wavering, was he seeking guidance? Or did he want to put it to a test? If so he should go further, should bring a girl and really test it. But for her it would have to be the islands. Blue sea. Sandy beaches. Lazy little villages with street cafes and curio shops. The teasing became a challenge. And the challenge became serious.

It was difficult and yet it was easy. For him everything was important, for her nothing was important. And so they planned it in a matter-of-fact way, as if they were merely embarking on a bus journey into Dublin. As soon as the graduation ceremony was over. A month. Starting in Crete. Then through the islands. Athens. And finally to Delphi.

Fonsie was irritated when he saw an elderly couple hovering about the tables outside. They shuffled through to the window and sat down in the shade of the awning. Damn. He propped his cigarette carefully on the edge of the ash-tray. Relieved when they ordered only two beers.

Greek music still playing when he sat down again. What was that fellow's name? His music had been banned by the Colonels. Zorba's music. Theodorakis. That was it. Theodorakis. His music had been banned and he himself had been exiled. Or had he fled the country? No matter.

When they arrived at the airport in Heraklion it was he who felt like fleeing the country. Back to the security of the seminary. Terror? Anxiety? Guilt? But there was no turning back. A knot in his brain, so that he couldn't think. A knot in his chest, so that he couldn't feel. A knot in his groin that threatened to ridicule his intentions. But she was relaxed. And that helped.

In the room at the pensión overlooking the harbour of Xania she slipped off her dress and hopped into the bed. Teasing him. Laughing at his awkwardness as he untied his shoes. She was frivolous as he fumbled to acquaint himself with her body. Suddenly they had made love. A rush of an affair. Full of excitement. With little of love, less of satisfaction. It was consummated. And over the following weeks they learned to take some pleasure from their mating.

They were on the ship out of Heraklion when they heard the news from another passenger. Trouble in Cyprus. Makarios had fallen. Turks had invaded. War between Greece and Turkey inevitable. Tourists fleeing as fast as boat or plane could carry them.

Huddling in a corner of the crowded deck they talked. The two of them. Decided to stay. Hundreds were waiting at Santorini, clamouring to board the ship. They were the only ones to disembark.

The elderly couple had finished their beers. Fidgeting. Looking around. Reluctantly Fonsie got up and went out to them again. Two more beers. They were Australian, he decided. Seldom any Irish in this area. Now and again. Like the Irish MEP that came in one night for his dinner. Afterwards he sat around. Drinking beer. All by himself. Fonsie had made a few remarks to acknowledge their common nationality. When the diners had thinned out, the MEP invited him to have a drink. Fonsie accepted. They ended up drinking and talking into the early hours. Talked nonsense mostly. He was from the south of Ireland and was reminiscing about great hurling matches between parish teams in Tipperary or Cork. Wherever. Not to let the west down, Fonsie came up with similar epic encounters in Gaelic football on the playing fields of County Roscommon. The more intoxicated they had become, the grander the scale of these titanic struggles. All nonsense. A crowd of lads togging out under a hedge. Someone with no togs at all pulling on a jersey, folding the legs of his trousers into his socks. Looking for the football. Did anyone remember to bring the football? Titans indeed. Only in the imagination. Only in the mist of nostalgia and intoxication.

The imminent war between the Greeks and Turks was like that. They were mobilising on the island of Santorini. Young men in khaki being sent forth by wailing mamas. Old men solemnly patrolling the streets on the back of pick-up trucks, ancient rifles slung across their shoulders. Shops closed. Offices closed. Banks closed.

That caught them on the hop. The banks being closed. No money. Not the best place to be stranded. On top of a volcano. True. The town was perched up on the top. Steps. Steps. Steps down to the sea. A donkey ride if you weren't watching your drachmas. Black sand on the beach. Like cinders. Hot too. Too hot for your bare feet. She didn't like the place. Wanted to leave. But all the ships were gone. Commandeered by the army.

It was a full week before they escaped. A ship arrived. Back servicing civilians. They boarded, and got off at the next stop. Paros.

Paros was a lovely island. Tender. She loved it. Lying out on the deserted beaches. Not a tourist left but themselves. Swimming in the warm waters of the Aegean. Back to the pension to make love. Dressing for dinner. Out on the open square. Moussaka. Kebabs. That sort of fare. Delicious. Afterwards sitting back. Drinking retsina or raki. Ruminating. Passive as the old men telling their worry-beads. He too liked the island.

But they had to push on. Mykonos. Briefly. Then to Lesbos. An agreed stop. He wanted it because it was the home of

Sappho, she because it was close to the Turkish coast. She wanted to see Turkey, even though she could not now visit it.

The two Australians were ready to go. They were married. He knew. They had not spoken to one another for the duration of two beers. Marriage was like that. Two horses harnessed to the one plough. Easier to pull together quietly and get on with the job. That much you learn. Fonsie's wife taught English to rich little Belgian kids. It was a job. She didn't like it. She didn't dislike it either. Tried it himself once. Once was enough. Tried other things too. Not much in the line of career opportunities for a theology graduate. Still. They earned a living between the two of them. Paid the rent. Bought food. Returned to Ireland twice a year. Might have been better off to have stayed in Ireland. Who knows? Seemed a good idea at the time. To go abroad. Adventurous. So it seemed.

Trip to Lesbos was an adventure. Raised eyebrows all round. Why Lesbos? The army was on Lesbos. Dangerous.

Nothing could have looked less dangerous than the army on Lesbos. Less heroic. Gawky youngsters in khaki loitering on the beach. All had been conscripted in a hurry, given a uniform and gun, sent to the front. The officers sitting around in the cafe downstairs. Detached. Bored. So silent Fonsie imagined they were listening to the creaking of the bed. A bit inhibiting. But whenever he looked out the window to check, there they were, legs stretched, gazing across the water at the Turkish coast. Some of them had English. Not much. Less information. Rumours, they explained, with a shrug. Rumours of fighting in Cyprus. Rumours of fighting in Thessaly. Rumours of a mutiny in the army.

Then. Suddenly. It was as if the Turks had finally landed. Deafening gunfire. Shouting. Screams.

Running to the window. Peeping out. Bedlam down below. Officers dancing. Throwing their arms around one another. Kissing. Hugging. Soldiers running wildly about the beach. Shooting into the air.

Chasing down to find out what had happened. The Colonels, they said. The Colonels had fallen. Gone. Euphoria. Men laughing. Men weeping. They joined in. Such drinking. Dancing on the sand. Zorba's dance or a drunken imitation of it. Singing. Songs that had been silenced for years. They were free. They could sing what they wanted to sing, think their own thoughts, express what they felt. The bonds were broken. They were free.

Bliss to be among them at that moment.

The ship sailing for Piraeus the following day was ablaze with flags. Music blaring from the public address speakers. Everyone drunk. Including them. Dancing on the deck. Dancing in the cafeteria. Dancing everywhere.

In Athens the streets were packed. Thousands upon thousands. Waving flags. Singing. Chanting slogans.

That night they went to a concert in the Amphitheatre. The banned songs were greeted with rapture. Musicians who had not been heard in public for a generation were paraded on stage. Acclaimed. All their curtain calls in one.

That night he decided to leave the Church. Freedom. The breaking of bonds. That was the essence of living. It could never be the same again. For Greece or for him.

The telephone rang. Fonsie looked at his watch before answering it. Sometimes his wife rang in the afternoon. After she returned from school. If there was a problem. The telephone was her only line of communication to him, she frequently complained. True. At least for five days of the week. She left in the early morning. For school. With the children. Not children any more. Almost finished. Soon for college. He didn't return until night. Every Sunday off. Every second Saturday. It was fine.

Not his wife on the phone. Just the owner. Checking whether he could work later that night. Had agreed.

Mount Parnassos was as awesome in reality as it had been in his imagination. The sweep of those mountain slopes. The fresh smell of trees as they climbed towards Delphi. Eucalyptus? Olive groves at intervals. She didn't take to it at all. On the bus from Athens to Itea she complained of the heat. Oppressive. Not like the islands. They should have stayed on the islands, she grumbled.

But this was what he had come for. And he was not disappointed.

She had a problem with the flies. Mosquitos, perhaps. Then she tired of the climb. There was a picnic table in the shade of a fig tree. She decided she would sit there and wait for him. He was relieved.

Alone on the slopes of Mount Parnassos. Where kings and warriors had climbed. To consult the oracle. To learn the truth. The sacred mountain of Apollo. Of the muses. Where the priestess breathed the vapours rising from the Underworld. And told men what they needed to know. But only the wise could puzzle it out.

Standing among the columns in the temple of Apollo he felt he could see all of Greece. The ships plying the channel towards Corinth. The mountains of the Peloponnese beyond. All of Greece. And it was now free. It was dancing. Singing. The bonds were broken.

He could have stayed there the rest of the day. The rest of the year. Forever. Searching for the cleft and the inspirational vapours of the Underworld. But he had to get back. She was waiting. At a picnic table. Impatient.

Nevertheless. He had been to Delphi. Learned the truth. Stood on Mount Parnassos and saw Greece young again and beautiful, shimmering beneath a blue veil, awaiting revelation. Full of hope. And possibility.

They didn't talk much on the way back to Athens. He was full. Mount Parnassos inside him. Afraid to dissipate it in uncongenial conversation.

In Athens he saw her off at the airport. Deferred his own flight. Wanted to stay in Greece, he told her. For a while. To sort out his mind. Wouldn't be returning to the Church. That much was certain. Everything else was in the realm of possibility.

Or so he thought. Another month he spent. Wandering about. Back to Crete. To locate a hippy colony on the south coast. Living in caves. Old Roman tombs. Liked the idea. But they played volleyball on the beach all day. Every day. And talked of nothing but how cheaply they could survive. Not the free spirits he was looking for.

Back through the islands. But it wasn't the same. Hated eating alone in the evenings. Missed her presence in the warm darkness. Lay awake contemplating the undulations of her body, the intimate crannies, the secret nooks of pleasure, the little spots of concentrated sweetness.

And Greece had changed. Again. Back to normal. Normal! No more explosions of joy. No more dancing in the streets. No more singing. Except to entertain the tourists in the cafes. Yes, the tourists were returning. Everything was back to normal.

In Dublin he telephoned her. Met her. Asked her to marry him. Provided they travel - that was his one condition. She agreed. Suggested Brussels to start. She had just been offered a teaching job there.

The rest is silence, as the man said. When the truth is revealed to you at Delphi, you ignore it at your peril.

BIKE

THE WOMEN OF THE HOUSE HELD A meeting. They decided that some things had to go. My wife, her two sisters, and my two cousins decided that the house was becoming cramped. They were right, of course. Add a male partner and an average brood of three children to each of those five females, and you will begin to understand the problem - all crammed into one house. I must clarify that it is a big Georgian house in Leeson Street, three stories over basement, with high ornamented ceilings in every room; yet the concentration of so many people into it gave the effect of a tenement - it is probably the only tenement in modern Dublin!

I don't own the house and I don't know who does. It was, so to speak, dropped in my lap. When I first came to Dublin, to take up a menial clerical position - a position I have occupied to this day - I rented the room on the ground floor inside the front door. The rest of the house was similarly let to students and young professional people, as they were described in the letting advertisements, and the Landlord called every Friday evening between seven and eight o'clock to collect the rent. As I was so conveniently situated inside the front door and always about on a Friday evening, not having been a drinker in those days, a practice grew up whereby other tenants left their rent with me as they exited for their weekend carousals. I became an unofficial rent collector for the Landlord, who neither thanked me nor rewarded me for my services. We never engaged in conversation while he took the money and counted it. I never even knew his name.

Then he stopped coming. One Friday night he failed to arrive, and I never saw him again. The other tenants continued to leave their rent with me, something that worried me enormously, especially when the money began to overflow the drawer in my sideboard. In fear of a robbery, I opened a bank account and deposited all the money I had collected, including my own rent. For several years this continued. And, according as tenants left, they handed their keys to me. I was prepared to accept responsibility for minding the rent money, but not for re-letting, so eventually I was living alone in an empty Georgian house.

That was when I decided to get married, and took a wife. She moved in with me to my room and enjoyed the thrill of the empty old house for a while. Unfortunately, she soon grew lonely and prevailed upon me to allow her mother and two sisters join us. There were so many empty rooms at the time that I had no logical basis for an objection. So they joined us. In time the mother died and the two sisters got married. Their husbands moved in as well. With three couples breeding, the house began to fill with little ones. Then two of my cousins came to Dublin to work in the Civil Service and I let a room to them. I was glad of this little private income at the time because I had commenced the practice of drinking. However, when these two got married they persuaded me to give them a second room, and they stopped paying me rent altogether.

With the proliferation of human life in the house, it was not surprising that the women complained of cluttering. The council of war demanded that I consign to the dump all the junk that was lying around. To make it convenient for me, they produced a notice from the Corporation that its disposal teams would be making a special collection of Household Junk on the following Tuesday. This notice came once a year and it had always been used in attempts to pressurise me into getting rid of the many old artefacts that had come into my care along with the house, objects such as broken armchairs, a Victorian hall-stand with shattered mirror glass, and, particularly, the old bicycle that was parked on the landing of the first floor. My reluctance to dispose of these items did not stem from any sentimental streak in my nature nor from any attachment to the antique; it stemmed from my overwhelming sense of responsibility for all that I was holding in trust, and my overwhelming dread that one day the Landlord would return and expect to find the house exactly as he had left it. My anxiety to maintain the role of faithful custodian was even more acute, since I no longer had the accumulation of rent to hand over to the Landlord on his return. Ever since my two cousins had ceased paying me rent, I had been making withdrawals from the bank account to finance my custom of drinking ale in the evenings.

However, on this occasion the women made a more aggressive assault than usual on the old rusty bicycle. They claimed that the children were constantly crashing into it and gashing themselves; they claimed that some day one of the children would die of tetanus or another unspeakable disease, and that it would be my fault because I didn't shift the rusty old bike.

Convinced, partly by their argument and partly by the thought that I might be able to sell the crock for the price of a few pints of ale, I concluded an agreement with the women: I would dispose of the bike, on condition that they did not press me to interfere with any of the other items on their hit-list.

Bald William, the local grocer, obliged me by putting my "For Sale" notice in his window, and within a few days I had a response, a telephone enquiry, an interested customer. I had to give her precise detail of every part, from the size of the wheels to the shape of the mudguards, and she seemed in no way put off by my frequent mention of rust. When I described the extended height of the handlebars emerging from the long neck in the frame of the bike, she became quite breathless.

"A High Nellie! Is it really a High Nellie?"

I had never heard of such a model, but assured her that it was, since it seemed to be a good selling point.

She arrived the next morning to inspect the bike. She was pushing a buggy into which was strapped a tawdry but healthy-looking girl-child of one year or thereabouts. Following her was a slim nubile girl of nineteen or twenty. The woman herself was of indiscriminate age, but old enough to be an unlikely mother of the infant. The nubile girl sat on the granite steps pushing the buggy to-and-fro while I fetched the bike for inspection. In the glare of daylight it looked a sorry sight indeed, the prevailing rust having reduced the chrome parts and the once-painted frame to the one dirty brown colour and the same rough texture. I now despaired of striking a bargain, even though I had previously pumped the wheels and ensured that it was functioning in all the expected ways. I decided I would settle for the price of four pints, my usual night's quota, if she would be prepared to take it off my hands.

She went into rapture when she saw it.

"It is. It is. A genuine High Nellie," she exclaimed. I thought perhaps I might have a week's drinking after all.

She examined it, back and front, top and bottom, with as much reverence as if it had been ridden by St. Patrick when he was chasing the snakes, or by Brian Boru when he was routing the Norsemen. She certainly didn't play a cool hand when it came to bargaining.

"I never thought I'd see one again," she said earnestly. "My first bike was a High Nellie. It was my present for my fourteenth birthday. I went everywhere on it. When I came to Dublin I brought it with me. I cycled it for years. Then it was stolen. I could never bring myself to buy another bike."

"Would you like to take it for a spin, and try it out?"

"Could I? I'll just ride around the block. Lisa will keep an eye on Annmarie." She nodded in turn at the nubile girl and the infant.

I carried the bike down the stone steps, handed it to her, and held the gate open to allow her the liberty of the streets.

She mounted the bike as if she had never sat on one before, but when she had gained her legs she pedalled with confidence down the road.

I went back to make small talk with Lisa. She was very pretty with a delicately-cut oval face and tightly-cropped black hair. She was ornamented with a diamante stud in her nose. She was a student of theology, she told me, in from the country. She had been sent by her parents to the home of Phyllis and her husband, in reply to an advertisement in a local paper; the arrangement was that she performed a certain amount of child-minding and domestic duties in return for accommodation and meals. She spoke with a quiet but assured voice. Her choice of theology as a discipline was easily explained. She was not preparing for a church career, nor was she a devotee of any particular religion. She was sent by her family to study at the University, but when her academic qualifications were assessed she was offered a place only on the course for which there were few takers - theology.

Annmarie had begun to whinge a little and Lisa was pushing her gently to-and-fro, humming soothingly to her.

I was very taken with the girl, and enjoyed our little discussion very much, even if I was on edge looking up the street and down the street for Phyllis's return. The small talk was exhausted, and I tried out a few theological topics, the existence of angels and the usefulness of the Mandala for achieving spiritual enlightenment. When the second hour had passed and I had begun to feel out of my depth in our discussion of the phenomenology of the spirit, my patience expired, and I decided to go and look for Phyllis. I told my wife to take Lisa and Annmarie inside and give them some tea and bread. Afraid that they would take flight as soon as my back was turned, I was determined to hold them as hostages until I got my bike back, or the price of it.

I got her address from Lisa and set forth. My first worry was that she had met with an accident, caused perhaps by a mechanical failure of the bicycle, and I wondered what my liability would be in such circumstances. I called at the police station and at the hospital, but there was no report of an accident.

I then called at her own address, surmising that she had been unable to re-trace her steps to my house - an unlikely explanation, as I lived on one of the main thoroughfares of the city.

Her husband answered my knock. He stood squarely in the door, dressed in shirt and trousers, in stockinged feet. His stomach pouted above his taut belt. There was a strong suggestion in his contrary expression that he had been roused from a nap. I explained my predicament. He scratched at his bald head and down the back of his flabby neck as if he were searching for some elusive itch. He didn't appear concerned, just annoyed in an intensely petulant way.

"Damn the woman anyway. She's getting sillier by the day." He spat out the words in no particular direction. He offered no further comment on the situation. I grew uneasy. Anxious to withdraw from this confrontation, I decided to cut my losses.

"I suppose I had better send the child and Lisa back to you."

"Damn the child. If she gave it to you, then you keep it. But send Lisa back to me. I want Lisa back, do you hear?"

I muttered a goodnight and withdrew. This was certainly a dilemma.

Night had fallen by the time I returned home. I found Lisa and Annmarie still sitting in the kitchen waiting for their crux to be resolved. The hostages had become refugees. I explained to Lisa, as diplomatically as I could, that Phyllis had hijacked my bike and had abandoned the two of them; they were not wanted by her husband, either - I simplified this aspect of the crux, as I was certainly not going to surrender Lisa, unless I was ridding myself of the child as well.

I got ready the spare room in the basement, the only unoccupied space in the house, which I kept in reserve for the occasional visits by my relatives from the country. I installed Lisa and the baby. They would be comfortable there, and the women of the house would see to their needs. It would take me some days to decide on a course of action, as I seldom made a good decision in haste.

The following night I consulted a drunken judge who patronised the same pub as I did. He seemed to think that I had entered into a contract, had acquired some assets, and was entitled to liquidate them. When I asked him for some suggestions as to how I might liquidate my assets, he became totally incoherent, laid his head on the counter, and began to snore. I could sell the baby on the black market. There were stories of small fortunes changing hands in such deals. That was a real possibility. I wondered what she would fetch. What then would I do with Lisa? Sell her too? But then white slavery was so much out of fashion in Europe. Unless I did something quickly I would be at a considerable loss, as they both had healthy appetites.

The more I thought about the problem, the more muddled

my mind became, the more my sense of grievance against Phyllis gnawed at my spleen. I was riled by the ever-present awareness that she had bested me. I imagined her gloating over her success, laughing in scorn at my gullibility. Her image haunted me night and day, so that I finally recognised I had only one course of action open to me, to track her down and force her to compensate me for the lodgings in addition to paying a substantial price for my bike.

Living in the centre of the city has its advantages. You strike up relationships with all kinds of interesting people, such as winos, newspaper sellers, the skinheads in Stephen's Green. It was to this network of friends that I now had recourse. I had difficulty in formulating a clear picture of Phyllis, but I had no problem describing the bike. And it was the bike that my friends succeeded in identifying. Within hours reports of sightings began to flow back to me. All over the city it was being spotted - fleeting glimpses of it careering down thoroughfares, disappearing around corners, emerging from side-streets, always being pedalled vigorously by a woman, sometimes described as middle-aged, sometimes as young, sometimes simply as a woman.

For two or three days I did nothing but try to correlate the information that was coming back to me through my network. No pattern was emerging, and I could only marvel at her energy and wonder how soon she would collapse.

She didn't collapse, but she certainly started to slow down. Sightings were now beginning to cluster and concentrate in the Temple Bar area, the new bohemian quarter of the city. The bike was being spotted chained to a lamppost outside a public house or being walked up the cobbled streets after closing-time. It was time to move in for the kill.

Temple Bar was one area of the city that was unfamiliar to me, and I made my way slowly and cautiously from pub to pub. The patrons were invariably young, and casual looking, making it all the more difficult for me to be inconspicuous. I dressed like the natives, in blue jeans and plaid shirt, and usually slouched on a high stool by the bar conducting monosyllabic conversations with the barman.

My guile and perseverance eventually brought success. Lurking in a pub early one evening, I saw her tethering the bike to the railings outside. I was petrified. I felt like a hunter across whose path a magnificent deer has strutted so close as to make a mockery of shooting. She came in the open front door, exchanged a greeting with the burly bouncer who was picking up glasses and re-arranging the chairs where people had just left. She walked past me over to a corner of the lounge; three women welcomed her with animated voices. From the corner of my eye I watched her every move. She sat down with her back towards me and ordered a pint of Guinness when the lounge girl approached. After a few minutes I took my own pint and sauntered over to occupy a vacant seat behind her, between her and the door.

One of the women had just attended a lecture on Existentialist philosophy and she was filtering her newly acquired wisdom through to the others, pausing regularly to imbibe more Guinness.

"You can do whatever you want to do," she declared in a high-pitched voice that trembled from intoxication. "You can be whatever you want to be. It's a simple matter of choice."

"Absolutely true," agreed Phyllis taking a slurp from her pint. "You can do anything you want."

'Not on my bike, you can't,' thought I, 'and not while I'm feeding your child and your child-minder.'

After a while her three companions got up to leave. In turn they embraced her.

"Good luck, Phyllis. Have a nice trip."

Where was she going? I was seized by panic. When she sat down again she re-located herself with her back to the wall. She was now sitting alongside me, and couldn't avoid noticing my stare as she watched her companions depart. She glanced at me in half-recognition as if I were some face from her distant past. I sensed that she did not associate me with an event that was not yet a fortnight old. Perhaps my clothes or the changed surroundings had dulled recognition. Or perhaps she had lost all control of her faculties!

I nodded at her and edged closer along the bench seat. She

became slightly nervous, but held her ground. Whether it was because of her hair, which she now wore loose, or because of her heightened complexion induced by alcohol and all that physical exertion, she certainly appeared much younger than she did on our last encounter.

I passed a compliment on the pub, to which she nodded her agreement. I still could not determine whether she recognised me or not. There was silence once more.

Then she turned squarely and emphatically to me. "Isn't it marvellous what they're doing with Temple Bar?"

"Yes, marvellous, indeed," I agreed, without the remotest idea as to what marvellous things she was referring.

"It really has such character, and it's so alive now. It's marvellous."

"Yes, marvellous," I agreed again.

"We miss out on so much of life. It's so important to have a place like this at the heart of the city, pulsing with life, full of people, exploding with ideas."

"Yes, yes, absolutely essential."

"Everywhere you turn in Temple Bar you find people expressing themselves, in music, in art, in writing, or just in the sheer joy of living."

"Are you involved in the arts yourself?"

"No, unfortunately," she laughed, and took a deep swig out of her pint. "I'm involved in the joy of living."

"But you must do something. What about work? Family?"

"I'm finished with all of that," she declared, as if a cloud had appeared on the horizon, but a cloud she was not going to allow overshadow the sunshine in her mind. "I'm off on a long trip. I'm catching the boat tonight. Holyhead. I'm going to cycle from there to the south coast of England, down through the Wye Valley and Somerset, places like that, places I've always wanted to see. And it's so easy on a bike. You just sit up and keep pedalling. From the south coast I'll catch a ferry to France. Then down to Paris! I'll spend some time there, a week, maybe two. Off again down to the Alps, Italy, Florence, Rome. Were you ever in Rome?"

"No," I replied, and in truth had never experienced the

slightest desire to go there, always associating the place with pilgrims and the Pope flapping his arms from his top window.

My reaction to her eulogy was one of vast and intense resentment, so vast and so intense that it took me by surprise. How dare she? The sheer effrontery of it! It wasn't just the bicycle she had stolen from me; it wasn't just her tricking me into assuming her responsibilities; it was the audacity of the woman. She had no right to do these things, no right even to think such thoughts. It was a threat, an insult to me in a way that was too deep to articulate, too deep even to fathom.

"Rome must be marvellous," she rambled on, patently unaware of my dark thoughts, unaware of the stool I had slowly edged across her direct path to the front door." All those paintings, and sculptures, and buildings! Isn't it fascinating to think that, once you land on the coast of France, there is a road all the way to Rome. In the days of the Empire they used to say that all roads lead to Rome. Now there is at least one road that leads to Rome, and I intend to cycle every inch of it."

"Will you stop there? Will you come back then?" I asked, wondering at what stage she planned to resume her responsibility for her child.

"Not at all," she was quite peremptory. "From Rome I will go down to Brindisi, and there catch a boat for Greece. I believe the islands are marvellous, especially Crete. And there are very few cars, so it will be ideal for cycling."

"And I suppose from Greece you will go on to Turkey or Egypt."

"I hadn't thought of that. But you're quite right. A person should see Istanbul, and the Pyramids too."

"After that the Himalayas, and India!" She looked at me sharply when she detected the tone of cold mockery in my voice. I launched a direct assault.

"What about your daughter? Are you going to put a chair-seat on the back of the High Nellie and bring her with you? Are you going to pay me for my bike before you wear it out on the highways of Europe?"

She continued staring at me as if she were trying to make sense of my outburst. Then she stood up indignantly. I stood up just as indignantly, determined that she should not escape this time. My knee was firmly behind the stool that was blocking her flight-path. As the bike was chained to the railings, she had no hope of shaking me off in any event.

"I am going to the toilet," she declared in an aggrieved tone, and planked her hand-bag down on the table. I slowly sat down again. She could hardly set out for Rome without her handbag. Nevertheless, I eyed her closely as she made her way to the toilet, and didn't take my eye off the toilet door while she was inside.

Eventually she emerged. She went straight over to the bouncer who was lounging at a table talking to patrons. She tapped him on the shoulder and I watched him bend his ear to her and then turn to stare at me while he listened to whatever tale she was telling him. He nodded seriously, his brows tightening around the glare he had directed on me.

Then she swaggered over, followed purposefully by the bouncer. She grabbed her bag from the table without saying a word. Her bearing, her swagger said everything, said that she had won the battles and the war without a single formidable engagement.

As she turned to leave, the bouncer put his hand roughly on my shoulder.

"You stay there," he snarled. "Or, if you insist on leaving, you and I will take a few steps down to the police station. It's a damn shame that a young lady can't enjoy the freedom of this town without being troubled by your likes."

I sat back in a state of dismay. The 'young lady' was quickly outside, unchaining the bike, mounting it, and cycling down the street so fast that her hair was blowing behind her. Somerset, the White Cliffs, Paris, Rome - how dare she? In the following minutes I made several attempts to rise, hoping to head her off at the ferry, but each time I was arrested by a threatening glance from the bouncer. Eventually it was too late. She had given me the slip. I lapsed into a night of heavy drinking.

When I finally drank my head clear, I spent several hours contemplating my predicament. My first instinct was to follow her without delay, on the next ferry, through England, through France, Italy, wherever she went, as a weasel follows a hare, never wavering, never losing determination, until I nailed her, devoting the rest of my life, if necessary, to the task of thwarting her.

But, a few pints later, my reasoning had come full circle. I decided to let her go, to let her away with the damned bike, and to forget her. There was no point in letting the injury fester. I would keep Lisa and the child. The house was big enough, the room was free, and my relatives never called anyway. I would give up drinking and take an interest in theology. I could have long discussions with Lisa in the evenings instead of going to the pub; that would save enough money to support her and the child. I might even marry her. Why not? In my house who would notice another wife, another family? If Lisa had any scruples we could both convert to one of those religions that allowed bigamy. Why not? Wasn't it Phyllis who said you could do anything you wanted to do?

Requiem for Johnny Murtagh

I WAS NOT SPEEDING. I WAS CRUISING ALONG and almost home. Three and a half hours out of Dublin, and I was within five miles of my destination. One moment I had an open stretch of country road in the long beam of my headlight, the next his grotesque face and wildly waving arms filled the windscreen. I drove the brake-pedal into the floor and stiffened behind the wheel. The tyres gripped and gave an almighty drag against the car. There was no frost on the road, no water. Even so, I didn't stand a chance. There was a thud as I rammed him below the belt, and a louder thud as his head smashed downwards on the bonnet. There he rested until the car skidded to a halt. I jumped out and turned him over on the bonnet. He was moaning. So he was still alive.

I screamed at him, "How did you get in front of me? How did you get there?" He just kept moaning, and the only coherent words I could make out were, "Can't sleep." I looked up the road, and down the road. There wasn't a wisp of car-light coming from either direction. What would I do? I was in a frenzy. There was no house for half-a-mile on either side. What should I do? The rules of thumb were easily recalled. Telephone the police. Call an ambulance, a doctor, a priest to administer the last rites for fear he should die. Never leave the scene of an accident.

There wasn't a police station for fifteen miles, nor a telephone that I knew of for at least a mile. Anyway, how could I leave him there to go for help? He was still sprawled across the bonnet, muttering, "Can't sleep. Can't sleep." I had recognised him, of course, Johnny Murtagh, the second his face flashed in the headlight, even though I hadn't laid eyes on him for several years. He was noted for his eccentric habits. Ever since he left the primary school he had withdrawn from the company of his peers, and continued to live with his mother in their little three-roomed cottage. And what a cottage! It was one of the most forlorn sights on the landscape. While other families built bright new homes, the Murtagh cottage got more and more bedraggled. It was reputed to be filthy inside, and Johnny had all the appearance of such a lifestyle.

His face was black with dirt, and his old clothes were similarly caked with grime. I couldn't make out whether he was bleeding or not. I decided to do the only thing that seemed sensible. I rolled up my overcoat and made a pillow on the back seat. As gently as I could, I lifted him off the bonnet and edged him into the car.

"Johnny, I'm going to take you to the hospital. Are you in much pain?"

"Can't sleep."

What if his back was broken? Or his neck? What if his skull was fractured? I was terrified. What if he died in my car on the way to Sligo? I caught his chin and shook his head gently.

"Johnny, Johnny, open your eyes. Do you recognise me?"

To my relief he did open his eyes. There was a wild and vacant stare, but he gradually focussed on my face.

"Peter Sullivan," he mumbled slowly.

"I knocked you down, Johnny. But it wasn't my fault. You came right out in front of me. You came at me from nowhere."

He nodded, as if agreeing.

"Don't worry. I'll get you to the hospital. You'll be all right."

I jumped into the driving seat, and turned the car quickly, back in the direction of Sligo town. Again I heard him muttering. "Can't sleep." Better to keep him awake, I thought, better not let him lose consciousness.

"What were you doing on the road, Johnny?"

"Can't sleep."

Scarcely half-a-mile down the road I hit the brow of the little hill above Farranaharpy. The sudden bounce made Johnny cry out and I slowed down. He was certainly in pain. It is perhaps twenty miles from Templeboy to the town of Sligo and there are many humps and hollows on the road. Not Hell's flags would have been more painful to traverse than the road to Sligo that night, with Johnny groaning in agony every time the car lunged. I tried to keep him talking, even though I had remembered it was a person with a drug-overdose you were supposed to keep conscious. While there were sounds out of him, he was at least still alive.

"We're in Skreen now, Johnny, just passing the creamery. Do you send milk to the creamery?"

"Can't sleep."

"Is it beef then, Johnny? Have you got a few cattle on the land?" I thought of the pitiable cluster of little fields that were his farm, growing more ragwort and thistles than grass.

"Can't sleep."

"What do you want to sleep for Johnny? No one pays you for sleeping. It's a waste of time."

"Australia."

I almost turned my head and caused another accident, I was so surprised by the suddenness of this new word.

"Australia. It's a fine country, Johnny. I've never been there. I wouldn't mind going sometime. On holidays. I wouldn't emigrate or anything. Would you like to go to Australia, Johnny?"

"When I sleep."

"What do you mean by that, Johnny?"

"Australia. When I sleep."

"Ah, yes. You dream of Australia when you're asleep."

"No dream. Wife, child, house, Australia, sleep."

"I don't understand, Johnny. You have a wife, a child, a house, in Australia when you're asleep?"

"Yes."

"And that's why you want to go to sleep so badly?"

"Yes."

His wits were certainly forsaking him, but I was relieved to have him talking.

"Tell me about Australia, Johnny. What is your wife's name?"

"Annie."

"Is she pretty?"

"Yes. Blonde. " And I could detect a warmth in his tone despite the painful gasps that he gave with every syllable.

"And your child. Is it a boy or a girl?"

"Daphne."

"We're well on the way, Johnny. Those are the street-lamps in Ballisodare you can see now. And, tell me, do you have a job in Australia?"

"Builder's yard."

"That must be hard work, carrying bags of cement and the like. But I suppose you are well paid. Did you say you have a house?"

"Bungalow. Nice."

"Australia is a big country, I believe. What part of Australia do you have your house in?"

"Geraldton. North of Perth."

By then I had reached the grounds of the hospital. I drove straight up to the casualty door, halted in front of it, and ran inside to get help. I explained to the orderlies how the accident had happened as they deftly lowered him on to a stretcher. I followed them inside and took a seat in the cubicle until the doctor came. After a rapid examination, while I again recounted the details of the accident, the doctor declared: "We'll have to get him to the theatre right away." Alone again, I stood over Johnny, looking down into his face.

"They're taking you to the operating theatre," I said. "They will look after you. And I'll wait around to see how you get on, so that I can tell your mother."

He didn't respond for a moment. Then he looked up at me with a pleading glance.

"Ring her for me. "

"Who, Johnny?"

"Annie, in Australia."

"Sure, Johnny, sure I will. What's her number?"

"726514. Geraldton."

I took out my cigar box and wrote the number on it.

"What message will I give her, Johnny?"

He paused and thought.

"Tell her I'll be back."

"Fine, Johnny. I'll ring this number, speak to Annie, and give her your message."

"Promise."

"I promise."

The orderlies had come to wheel him away at this stage. As he was moving out of the cubicle he cast me a slightly sheepish grin through the distortions pain had wreaked on his swarthy features.

"Peter," he said.

"Yes, Johnny."

"They call me John in Australia."

Whatever they might do for his poor broken body, I thought the medical profession would have an even greater problem putting to rights his poor deranged mind. I went outside to be in the open air, to be alone, possibly to be in the direct line of vision of the Almighty. For, if ever I was close to praying, I was close to it that night. The car I had abandoned was obtrusively close to the door, so I sat in and drove it around to the visitors' parking area. Craving a little comfort, I lit a cigar and smoked it slowly. Through the windows of the wards on the ground floor I could see the nurses tending their patients. It seemed an intimate little world, self-contained, but totally remote from where I sat isolated in the car park. Having sucked whatever consolation I could from the cigar, I returned to the Casualty Ward, and waited. It was perhaps an hour later that the doctor came looking for me.

"I have bad news," he said solemnly. "He died before we could do anything. He had severe internal injuries. I'm sorry. Will you inform the next-of-kin? And of course you will have to report it to the authorities."

I was in a daze as I left the hospital. I was in a daze as I gave a detailed account of the accident to the police sergeant. I was in a daze as I drove back the long lonely road to Templeboy, wondering how I would tell Mrs Murtagh that I had killed her only son.

Approaching the door of the cottage I caught a glimpse of her through the window. She was sitting beside the fire watching television. She opened the door to my knock and then went back to lower the volume on the television set.

"I have bad news for you, Mrs Murtagh," I said.

She lifted her hand to her mouth. "It's Johnny," she gasped. "Isn't it?"

"It is, Mrs Murtagh. He's been in an accident."

"Oh, God. He's not dead, is he?"

I paused for a moment to let the suspicion of my awful tidings take root in her mind.

"He's dead, Mrs Murtagh."

She knotted her fist and stuck it so far into her mouth, I thought she would swallow it. She curled into the armchair and buried her head in the crook of her arm.

"I'm sorry, Mrs Murtagh," I said, desperate to say or do something, and I sat into another armchair on the opposite side of the fire. The house deserved its reputation for squalor. Every detail, from the pock-marked blistering paintwork to the tattered vinyl covering on the floor, contributed to the overall effect. There were dirty saucepans and broken mugs arrayed on the dresser. And the kitchen table was loaded indiscriminately with items of food and used dishes.

"How did it happen?" she asked eventually, between sobs. I explained exactly how the accident had occurred. She didn't blame me.

"Sure God knows it wasn't your fault. Whatever way his wits were rambling, poor Johnny mustn't have known where he was."

"He kept repeating that he couldn't sleep, as if he were demented."

"He turned strange lately, sure enough," she nodded.

"But what was his problem with sleep?"

"He was a great sleeper until a couple of weeks ago. Sometimes he worried me, he would sleep so long. He might go to bed at eight or nine o'clock, and still he wouldn't rise till twelve or one the next day. It was unnatural. And I declare to God it was impossible to rouse him when he was asleep. I often roared at him and pulled at him, but to no avail. Not an eye would be open. So I left him to his ways, sleeping longer and longer. Then, some time recently, I noticed he was having trouble getting to sleep at night. I used to hear him in his room, pacing around the floor, and coming out here sometimes to make a cup of tea. Tea was his great weakness, but wasn't it a small failing in one who neither smoked nor drank?"

"He mentioned Australia."

"Australia," she repeated slowly. "Yes, he had some notion about Australia. I often wondered if he was thinking of emigrating. He used to tear out any little piece from the newspaper where there was a mention of Australia. And the odd time he went into Sligo or Ballina he came back with an armful of magazines and brochures from the travel agents' offices, all about Australia. Come on and I'll show you where he had the full of a box beside his bed."

She led the way through the door into the bedroom and switched on a light. The smell of stale sweat was overpowering. She walked over the articles of clothing that were littered on the floor. His bed was an army-style bunk with a few grey and brown blankets thrown on top. She lifted the lid of a large timber box that stood by the head of the bed. I sat down to look inside. It was, as the old woman had indicated, filled to the brim with pages from newspapers, magazines, travel brochures. And, sure enough, they were all about Australia. I examined some of them. It was the usual - photographs of beaches, kangaroos, Aborigines, and Ayers Rock.

"Poor Johnny," she said. "Isn't it terrible to think that he's gone, and how he wasted his life either sleeping or lying here reading those old magazines."

I felt that I had at last reached an understanding of the unfortunate man I had killed, and I felt a great sorrow for a stunted life and the stunted lives of so many more like Johnny. The old woman would accept none of my offers of help. Nor did she want the company of any friends or neighbours for the night. So I left the house, having arranged to return in the morning to take her to the hospital.

My state of mind had improved somewhat as I finally began to drive the last few miles to Dromore West. I was not guilty. The old woman did not hold me responsible. I had done everything that a person could do or should do in such circumstances. But then the man's dying wish flashed across my mind. The telephone call. Of course it was only part of his strange elaborate fantasy. Wouldn't I be as big a lunatic as he if I were to go ringing a telephone in Australia? Still there was something solemn and binding about a promise made to a dying man, and I knew I would have no peace until I had kept my word.

I was approaching Quinn's pub and noticed it was still open despite the late hour. Knowing they had a public telephone, I wheeled in on the street. I was also drawn by the drink, and felt it would bring me some relief. Tom Quinn looked at me with curiosity when he had placed the double whiskey and the pint of beer on the counter in front of me.

"Are you all right?" he enquired. I told him of the accident. "The Lord have mercy on the dead," he said slowly, and, turning to the three men who were drinking at the other end of the bar, he informed them: "Peter here has been in an accident down the road. Poor old Johnny Murtagh is dead." The three of them gathered around me and, once more, I had to repeat the details of the accident.

"He kept saying that he couldn't sleep, as if that were the problem," I said, by way of reflection.

"If Johnny Murtagh couldn't sleep, it was a severe handicap to him."

There was a brief silence and then one of them burst into compulsive giggling. Another spluttered. Finally the three of them and Tom Quinn were all caught in a swell of uncontrollable laughter.

"He couldn't sleep. Sure the man had exhausted the quota he had been given for a lifetime." The incongruity of their laughter quickly helped to suppress it.

"We didn't mean any disrespect to the dead," explained Tom Quinn when they had finally re-assumed an appropriate solemnity.

"No disrespect at all to poor Johnny, probably the most inoffensive poor devil that ever wore shoe leather."

I knew these three men by sight, but I couldn't name them.

"Do you know if he had any friends in Australia?" I asked. "Or anyone he might have known that emigrated there?" Each of the four men thought deeply, but agreed with one another that there was no one from the locality who had gone to Australia, and Johnny was never known to have had any friends or acquaintances outside the locality.

"It's just that he asked me to call a number in Australia."

"That's strange, all right," said Tom. "But the only way you'll find out is to give it a ring."

I had swallowed the whiskey and was half-way through the pint of beer. The soothing effect of the alcohol was restoring me to my business-like self. I got Tom to give me the change of a ten-pound note in silver coins, and went out to the telephone box. The operator was remarkably quick, considering she was making contact with the other side of the earth. I heard her asking, "Is that Geraldton 726514?" Then, returning to me, she asked me to insert the coins and press the button.

"Could I speak to Annie, please?" I asked confidently.

"Yes, this is Annie speaking," came the reply in a lovely feminine Australian drawl. My confidence was demolished. I almost dropped the telephone. Why my blood didn't stop flowing at that moment I will never understand.

"Hello, hello," she called out when I didn't respond.

"I'm a friend of John Murtagh," I eventually managed to articulate.

"You're a friend of John's," her voice lifted with enthusiasm, "and you're from Ireland too, I can tell by the accent. John isn't here. In fact I'm very worried about him because I haven't seen him for the past two weeks. It's so unlike him to disappear like this." I was in a state of utter confusion. What was I to say? What was his message? - That he would be back! What sort of a message from a dead man was that to give to a woman? He didn't know he was going to die when he gave me the message. Did he? What kind of vortex was I getting pulled into?

"Your daughter," I queried tentatively.

"Little Daphne. Oh, she's fine, but she's missing her Daddy so much."

I could take no more.

"Listen, Annie," I said, "I'll phone back in a few days."

"Yes, do that. I'm sure he'll be back by then. And he will certainly enjoy hearing from an Irish friend."

"Thank you, Annie. Goodbye." I hung up the receiver and had to lean against the back of the box for a few minutes to try and regain my composure and my faltering hold on reality. After a while I ventured back to the bar and swallowed the remains of my beer, immediately ordering another pint and double whiskey.

"Well, did you get through?" asked Tom Quinn as he placed the drink in front of me. He refused payment. "It's on the house."

"Yes, I got the number all right. Someone answered, but they never heard of Johnny Murtagh."

"I'm not surprised that they never heard of Johnny in Australia," ruminated one of the men. "Sure if Johnny hadn't been famous for sleeping, we wouldn't have heard of him even here." I could sense the laughter welling up again, and felt that this time I might join in.

Turfman

STREET CLEAN, WINDSWEPT. CLAN BRASIL, sept of the otherworld. Nobody but me, and the wind, and her approaching form. Pub on the corner, haven, Headline.

Closer, moving between me and the pub, drawing eye, and mind, and soul, and body. Drift of yellow hair on the breeze. Womanshape sculpted by the hungry wind. Fingered and thumbed. Voluptuary.

Poise in movement. A bale of peat briquettes in either hand. Balance and harmony.

I gave her my eye, she gave me hers. Smiled.
- Would you carry my briquettes for me?
- Would I carry your Cross for Ireland, Lord? Would I what?

Bales lighter than mind. Not earth. Already fire and air, anticipating their imminent burning. But the odour is peat. Odour of bogs, of youth. Odour of wraiths and will-o-the-wisp. Odour of dreams.

And the fiddle waltz, with the fire, and the hearth-rug stretched for stretching. If God has not sent this woman, how can the Devil be so benign?

We talked of marvels, how a road can have the common sense to climb across the canal and scuttle off into the little streets of Harold's Cross, how the electric lamp has adversely affected the working conditions of ghosts, how a white knight cannot exist without a damsel in distress.

The wind blowing her drapes touched cloth against cloth. Sensations of touch. Joy. Bliss.

We arrived. Elphin grot. Key in the door. Opening to unspeakable pleasures.

Then a call. Sweet as a blackbird to her mate.

- I'm home dear.

Dispelled.

And what rough beast? Braces hanging about his haunches? Belly spreading over the couch? Waiting for her.

Bales of peat are earth once more. Weight. Pain. And two feet locked in the wet bog. Smell of bog on clothes, on hands. Stronger than the perfumes of Arabia.

Bales dropped.

Bogmen never die. Hell must seek them out and torture them with dreams.

Behind The Castle Walls

Every day she came, the girl with the golden blond hair and the eyes like sea-pools. Every day the Prince was watching for her, waiting for her. At first it was always difficult to pick her out among the scores of his subjects and the scores of tourists who thronged daily up the flights of steps to his castle walls. Then something caught his eye, the sheen of her hair lit by a glance of sunshine, or the graceful swing of her body as she made her way further up the steps towards his window than others cared to come. Her approach was deliberate, as if she were coming with a purpose, as if she knew he was watching. Then came that wistful look at the window, the look that wrung his heart. Sometimes she came so close he could gaze into those sea-pools she had for eyes and he could dream of wonders within.

Since the girl started coming to the window, the viewing room had become his favourite place. How glad he was now that he had insisted on this window being inserted in the stout walls of the castle. They had resisted, his counsellors. They had their anxieties. But then they had anxieties about everything. He had been resolute, however. He wanted to examine the life his subjects had bartered into. He wanted to see the bustle and hear the din as they pursued their small, confined, comfortable lives. He wanted to look down at their factories, and offices, and houses, where they were content to be busy toing and froing in the one spot like so many ants in an anthill. He wanted to look upon the city, where his authority was recognised but where his powers were redundant.

They had compromised, he and his counsellors. They agreed to the window, but specified that it be triple-glazed, once to keep out the cold and the rain, twice to keep out the sounds of the city, and the third time to protect the castle against any violent attack. Moreover, the outside plate was coated like a mirror so that he could see out but no one could see in, for no one was permitted to look on him. It was a compromise; he would have enjoyed hearing the sounds of the city or eavesdropping on the conversations of the tourists. But the counsellors had their legitimate concerns. Theirs was the difficult task of maintaining his authority among his subjects who no longer experienced any need of his powers. He acknowledged their concerns, and generally did not interfere in their task of managing this tenuous relationship.

There was a time when the city, its habits and customs, seldom impinged on his thoughts. But he could no longer ignore it. The castle itself was the physical manifestation of the border-line between the sphere of his authority and the sphere of his powers, with its face towards the city, its back to the open country. The city had never been allowed to spread behind the castle; but in front it had spread for miles. And his subjects had all flocked there, forsaking their native mountains and their wooded valleys, forsaking their ancient lifestyle with its customs and traditions, forsaking the awe and wonder with which they once regarded him and trading it for a sterile recognition of his authority.

Every day she sat on the decorative abutment that surrounded the base of the chestnut tree. She delicately spread out her elaborate lunch on the flat stone beside her. She always had bread, usually two small brown rolls, and salad with watercress and radishes and cucumber. Sometimes she had slices of spiced meat, sometimes little cubes of cheese and a small carton of yoghurt. He loved to watch her bite into the bread with her delicately honed mouth and teeth that resembled a string of pearls. Every now and then she would look up from her eating and glance at the window as though she were trying to see through. And all she could see was a reflection of herself!

Almost an hour she spent there every day before tidying up her remains and hurrying back down the steps towards the city. And every day the Prince felt wretched while he watched her depart.

Perhaps the counsellors had been right; perhaps it had been a foolish scheme to build this window. Yet the Prince could not regret his insistence, in spite of the gaping agony inside him.

He had been happier back in the days when he had no cause to concern himself with the city. It had been small, insignificant, compared to the rest of his realm. He had been conscious of it only as an ugly growth spreading from the shadow of the castle. Now it was so obtrusive, it was everywhere. It sprawled across the landscape in front of the castle. It was in the hearts and minds of his subjects who were drawn to it as chips of steel are drawn to a magnet. It had driven a crude wedge between himself and his subjects, and had quenched the glow of wonder that had once animated their lives.

Although they were irrelevant in the warren of streets where his subjects lived, the Prince still revelled in the exercise of his powers. It was his delight to transform himself into a cloud and let himself be borne by the breeze up and over the foothills behind the castle, then to descend to the earth again in the form of a skylark in a rush of melodic ecstasy, to shin through the crags of the high hills as an antelope or sprawl indolently among the succulent grasses of the river bed as a little green lizard. And he could commune with all of these creatures, sometimes through significant sound, touch, or look, but more often through mere presence - and that was the most complete most satisfying of all communication, to be totally at one with a creature just by being in its presence.

The Prince wished he could take the girl under his wing and fly with her over sea-cliffs, share the delight of dashing downwards into the sea-spray, turn into beads of spray on the tip of a breaker and be carried laughing happily together to the bed of shingle.

But that could not be. She was a daughter of the city, as alien to his world as he was to hers. There was a time when he was not alien to his subjects. There was a time when they recognised him in the playful whirl of wind that brushed their cheeks, in the sudden shaft of sunlight breaking through a clouded sky, in the bleat of the first goat-kid on the hill slopes. That was the time they lived among the trees and waterfalls. That was back in the mornings when they worshipped him. That was before the city drew them from the hills and valleys and sucked the sense of wonder from their souls.

Was it loneliness that was now arousing even in him a fascination with the city? Was it mere loneliness that had him so obsessed with this girl, her hair golden as an ear of corn, eyes deep and mysterious as sea-pools? What was her life? Where did she work, and eat, and rest? Had she yearnings for something more than the mundane routines of her existence? Above all, why did she come here every day to have her lunch beneath his window?

He wished he could go down and talk to her, or sit on the kerb beside her, feel the same cold oozing from the same stone as she did, even pick the crumbs that shook from her dress as she rose to go. How simple for him to hop down as a robin and pick those crumbs, yet it could not be: they had fallen on the wrong side of the maring, they had fallen within the confines of the city.

He wondered what she thought of him, what image his name suggested to her mind. It oppressed the Prince greatly to think that he of a thousand forms, he of the continual shape-changing, should be reduced in the minds of his subjects to some abstract concept of authority. How would the girl respond if he presented himself to her, not disguised as a leaf upon the chestnut tree, nor as a butterfly among the leaves, but as himself, as the Prince. What would she see? Would she shrink from the sight? Or would she respond with warmth to the vision? But it did not matter. It was impossible anyway. All he could do was expose one face, one aspect, of himself to the girl, and that would be to deny the myriad other faces and aspects. It would be a lie. His only limitation, his only taboo, was that he mustn't limit himself. If he exposed his true self to the girl, in whatever form, he would be confined to that image in her perception and in the perception of all to whom she communicated the image. And since he would have chosen one form and denied the others, he would be weighted down by that identity, hooked to it as a ship is hooked to a single spot by its anchor. His ability to assume a new shape as easily as the sun casts a new shadow would be greatly impaired. Yet there were times when the comfort of limitation attracted him with seductive appeal, times when he understood and sympathised with the urge of his subjects to bury themselves in the intimate security of their premature coffins. Was it the terror of loneliness that drove them thus? Was it the craving for companionship? Was it ...the girl?

He had to know about her; he had to find out why she came to his castle walls every day; he had to learn why she cast that wistful look at his window, why she gazed at it as if she ached to see through.

He had to find out about her; he had to find out what image drew her up those flights of steps. He summoned his attendant, the only human being who could look on him in one of his forms, the only human being to whom he spoke, by whom all messages were relayed between himself and his counsellors. He was a young man, as his predecessors were all young men, singled out from among his subjects by what was known as "the mark". The mark made him special, made them all special, these young men, endowed them for this peculiar service, called them to attend upon him for the small duration that was left of their lifetime. The mark was their doom as well as their glory; their weakness was their strength; they came to him carrying the burnt candles of their lives, and stayed to attend upon him and to be his messenger.

The attendant entered and bowed respectfully. The Prince beckoned him to approach the window.

"I want you to find out who that girl is, and why she comes to sit under my window every day. Ask one of the footmen to go around tomorrow at this time - for she always comes at this time - and question her."

His attendant stood transfixed, silent. Then he spoke slowly, as if every syllable were a leaden weight on his tongue. "It won't be necessary to send a footman, My Lord. I know the girl.

She is my beloved. When I left her she swore that she would come to the castle every day until she heard that I had ...passed on. I tried to reason with her, but she would not be dissuaded."

The words came like a volley of spears piercing the heart of the Prince. He had not anticipated that explanation. He had not imagined even the possibility of such an explanation. He had witnessed the glow of love in her face, and in his folly he thought it had burned for him. How the lonely heart can deceive itself!

He looked at the attendant, whose eyes were now riveted to the window, his gaze fixed on the girl outside who was nonchalantly sipping some beverage through a straw. So this pale face, these infirm limbs, this effete spirit, was the object of her devotion. He felt a sudden urge to annihilate the figure before him, to assume its shape and present himself in that guise to the girl outside. But it was no more than an urge. What purpose would it serve? If she was in love with this ailing youth, then she could have no yearning for the wild rustic delights that he had to offer.

"Would you like to return to her?" he asked presently.

The attendant jerked his head around, in delight, then just as suddenly re-assumed his sombre expression.

"Alas," he said. "I know it cannot be. But there is nothing on the broad earth I would prefer than to return and spend the last of my days with her."

"You know I have the power. I could send you back. But, if I did that, the cycle of ritual would finally be broken. All would be changed. And you would no longer bear the mark. You might be as healthy and as strong as any young ruffian on your city streets. Would she love you then? Think about it. Perhaps it was the mark in you that attracted her. Without the mark you may hold no interest for her whatsoever."

"That might be indeed. I know this is all mere speculation, and I have no wish to renege on the responsibilities for which fate has singled me out. But, if I were given the choice, I would return as a mongrel cur to lick her heels."

"Then return as a mongrel cur you shall," replied the Prince. "But do not worry. That shall be your guise for eloping from the castle. Once you enter the city bounds you shall recover your former shape."

The attendant stood bewildered, looking from the Prince to the window, from the window to the Prince.

"Now be gone," said the Prince with a note of impatience in his voice.

Alone again, he took a last look at the girl. She was finishing her meal. She looked even more beautiful in the light of loss; her cotton dress, royal blue with tiny white polka dots, accentuated the gold in her hair, the sun-tanned hue of her skin. Her knees were crossed, and she was leaning sideways on one arm. On the hand that curled around the edge of the kerbstone he noticed a ring. Did his attendant give her that ring? Did she promise to wear it forever? How would she feel when he bounced back to her, a healthy bumpkin? Would she be satisfied? Or would she be yearning for the mystery that was lost? If so, the Prince would not be there to witness it.

He had to retreat from the edge before he released the attendant, before he was imprisoned by the image, the definition, which the attendant would no doubt announce to the city, not knowing that he knew nothing. He imagined him returning, being surrounded by wide-eyed citizens, telling all - 'I have seen him of a thousand shapes, this is how he looks. I have known him whose nature is a mystery, this is how he is defined'. And because he had returned from the threshold of the otherworld, the citizens would think he was revealing some truth.

The girl had finished her meal. She arose, gathered her litter and put it in the bin beside her, gave a last lingering glance at the window, and turned to commence her descent.

It was over.

The Prince had to concentrate on other things now. Now that he was abandoning the last vestiges of ritual, he was subverting his own authority. His continued presence behind the fortified line that divided his domain from his dominion was pointless, was probably untenable. He was tired, weary of the long unrelenting pain of loneliness. His absence would make no difference to his subjects - what difference did his presence make?

And his counsellors would find a way of accommodating the new situation. It was in their interest to do so.

He would fly, as an eagle, into the mountains. He would make his abode among the tallest peaks, where only the lion and the wild mountain goat were intrepid enough to venture. There he would live where humankind would never trouble him, never unless they came in search of him, which was less than likely.

As the Prince took off from the battlements he looked down and saw the cook shooing a mongrel cur out the kitchen door. A footman opened a side-gate and, with the toe of his boot, sent the creature yelping through into the city.

AND WHAT IS THE THUNDER?

RUMBLE OF LAUGHTER THROUGH THE heavens. Ha. Ha. Ha. Nice one. Nice one. The gods are pleased. Bloated bellies wobble with delight. Mutters and mumbles of approval mix with other mouth noises as they chew upon their feast. They enjoy these little entertainments. They vie with one another for the general approbation. Only the one they call Surlyface refuses to display amusement. Look now, look now, says the one whose turn it is to entertain. The gods slowly adopt an attentive silence once more.

* * *

McCann in the mirror. Sterile. Toilet annex to the anteroom. Waiting. Consulting. Consultant. Damned places so clinical, so barren. Bit of dirt wouldn't go astray.

Thin. Getting thinner? Fat had melted off him that first time he was sick. Chubby jowls gone. Stubby legs gone. Bulging waist gone. Effortlessly. Transfiguration. Exhilarating. As if the curse of a lifetime had been lifted.

Sallow shading had matted into a deep tanned complexion. He smiles. Recollection. Back in the office, after that first bout of illness, they accused him of having taken a buckshee holiday in the sun. Slaggers all. But he could take the slagging now. Now he existed. People noticed him, looked at him. He was real. Live. A person.

Even she had looked at him. Curiously. As if she had never

seen him before.

Nobody had seen him before. Registrar. Fancy name for the siding he had been shunted into. Fetcher of files. Minder of old tomes. General gofor. Dogsbody. And life had passed him by. Youngsters on the way up. Dullards with enough cunning to avoid sidings. The world and his nephew, all progressing. But not McCann.

Accepted his fate. Finally. Became assimilated into the landscape. Became one with dog-eared volumes, with soiled folders, with over-grown files bursting through tired covers. And nobody noticed him. Developed a way of talking to him as if he were not really there. As if he were mechanical. A robot. Polite enough but no personal engagement. And he had developed a way of dealing with them in like currency.

But all changed that time he was out.

McCann continues to examine the new image. Feast for the eyes. Pulls a smile to see white teeth. Turns to examine profile. Satisfied. Flushes the toilet even though he hasn't used it. Returns to the waiting room.

Yes, all changed. Everyone coming up to him, asking how he was. They had been lost without him. Balderdash! Still it was pleasing. More pleasing when the girls spoke to him. What a life he had missed.

And his old rags hanging about him. But that was quickly rectified. Fashionable tailor. Did wonders. Cost a few bob. Worth it! Tweed jacket. Slacks. Silk shirt. Did wonders.

She noticed the change. After three years sitting across the room. Never sparing him a glance.

But he had looked at her. Watched, studied her. Knew her face. Her moods. Knew every visible inch. And from such details had pieced together a total image. A total woman. In his mind. Through long contemplation.

All changed. Smiled at him in the morning. Enquired how he was. Pleasant. More than pleasant. It was bliss. Times he felt so close. And she was flesh and blood. Not a phantom of his mind. So close. Times he felt a word might bridge the chasm. A drink? Dinner? Just like that. But his nerve had failed. Or he hadn't recognised the opportunity until it was gone. Or hoped the chasm might be eliminated by some eruption of the earth. Fat chance that the earth would move for him. Still he hoped for some miracle.

When this was over. It would be different. When he was cleared. He would be sure. Then he would. He would. Would.

Cleared. He had to be. He felt so well. Moving up in the queue. Next. Such glum faces. Something seriously wrong with them. Yes, he never felt better in his life.

Door opens. His name. Into plush office. Book shelves everywhere. Must read a lot.

Behind a huge mahogany desk, the Consultant. Another glum face. Must have problems too. Thumbs through papers.

- Test results. Not good. Not good at all. Big C. All over. Worse, gone to the liver.
- The liver?
- I'm afraid so.
- What now?
- Nothing.
- Nothing?
- No point. Operating would be useless.
- How long?
- Weeks. Maybe less. I'm sorry.

Back through the waiting room. Head high. Dazed. Dignity, dignity. Must not let the guard down. Into the toilet. Locks door.

Head over the handbasin. Feels like retching. Tries to retch. Fails. Wants to scream. Mustn't.

Head up. Looks in the mirror. Face of death. Clear as a pikestaff. Eyes dark, sunken. Cheekbones prominent. Skin yellow. Pestilence written all over it.

How could he have so deluded himself? All that attention. All that concern. Pity. They had read the signs. Read them true. Terrified of death - even another's. And she. Perhaps kindness, or pity. Not what he had thought. Not that at all.

* * *

Rumble of laughter through the heavens. Ha. Ha. Ha. Nice

one. Nice one. The gods are generous with their applause. My turn next. My turn next. But Surlyface raises his hand. He has never availed of his turn. So they slowly, reluctantly, defer to him. It's not over yet, he says, and with a smirk sits back to entertain his peers.

* * *

Bags of transparent liquid hanging all around him. Tubes trailing in every direction. Needles.

McCann recalls a cowboy film. Old Indian walks off into the wilderness to die. Some dignity about that.

Another shot of morphine to boost delirium. Shot in the head more merciful. Put an end to it. Quickly.

Visitors. Yes. Three minutes a go. Hello. How are you feeling? Goodbye. Gone. Like the Passing Parade.

And then ... she is standing there. She. Ruddy hair falling to her shoulders. Eyes soft, warm. Concern in every feature.

McCann, helpless, blinks, several times. Delirium? Imagination? Dreaming? Still there. Coming closer.

He raises his hand. Draped with a creeper. Like man rising from some pre-historic swamp. How he must look. Frightful.

She does not appear frightened. Comes closer. Reaches out. Those lovely slim fingers. Long finger nails. How he had admired those graceful hands. Watched them at work. Or curled under her chin. Or sifting her hair. Now they were reaching out to him.

Her fingers touch his fingers. First touch. Ever. Never even shook hands. Now he is certain that she is there. She raises his fingers to her lips. Kisses gently. Fondly.

McCann numb with joy. Could die now. But not yet. Not yet. She sits on the side of his bed. Still holding his hand. No words. Has he died unawares, gone to heaven? No. Still feels her flesh.

Three minutes like a lifetime. Are a lifetime. All his days have been but a prologue to this. Days of loneliness. Days of despair. Days of despising himself. All shrunk into a brief lead-in to this climax. He is grateful for his life's affliction, and, with all the power he can muster, he blesses his fate.

Three minutes up. Nurse tapping her on the shoulder. She gives a final gentle squeeze on his fingers, then lets them drop. And McCann is certain he sees a tear welling in her eye.

Slowly, gracefully as always, she picks her way through suspended plastic bags, tubes, monitors, the paraphernalia of dying.

McCann sinks back into his pillow. No longer afraid, no longer nauseated by the style of his departure. Looks out the window. Oppressive storm clouds clearing. Being routed by a bright wind from the west. He decides it will be a good day to die.

DISTRACTION

THORNTON WAS SITTING INSIDE HIS BIG window, trying to maintain surveillance on the poultry enclosure. But his eye and his mind kept wandering back to the page on which he was writing.

A red fox sauntered down from the hills, his eye fixed on the poultry enclosure. When he spotted Thornton he veered towards the window. Squatting on his haunches, he began scratching his right ear with his right forepaw, while he peered in.

Thornton unlatched the window and opened it slightly. "What are you doing there?" he enquired.

"Scratching my ear," replied the fox. "I must have caught a flea. I always catch a flea when I come near you people. Or I always feel an itch from an imaginary flea. One or the other."

"You won't deceive me with any of your tricks or stratagems, so take yourself off."

"What tricks? What stratagems? Why am I always accused of duplicity? My purpose is always clear, my methods direct. Take you, for the sake of comparison. What were you up to just now while you were lurking inside that window?"

"I was not lurking. I was keeping watch over the poultry enclosure. That is my responsibility. And I was also writing a song," replied Thornton. "A love song."

"For whom?"

"For my love, of course. She lives a long way from here."

"Why don't you go to her, instead of sitting here writing a song?"

"It's not as simple as that in our world. Firstly, I have my responsibility to keep watch over the poultry enclosure, and you, no doubt, would be delighted to take advantage if you found me absent. Secondly, she lives at a great distance, as I have said. But, if I were to travel towards her, a wall would begin to rise up between us. The closer I would get, the higher the wall would rise; by the time I was in her presence the wall would be totally insurmountable."

"Why not burrow under it?"

"It's not that kind of wall. It's insurmountable in every direction."

"It sounds a bit like my flea, all in the mind."

"Maybe it is. But the mind has walls sheer beyond anything ever constructed in stone."

"Perhaps it has, but it doesn't take a bulldozer to demolish them. They crumble like the Walls of Jerico before a trumpet blast. Ah ha. That is the purpose of your song, is it not? To flatten the Walls of Jerico."

"Perhaps it is."

"Very good. Sing it, and I will tell you whether it is likely to succeed."

"I can't sing."

"You are one sad fool. You haven't much of a chance then. Have you?"

"I suppose not."

"Who will sing it?"

"Someone. Anyone."

"To your love?"

"Perhaps."

"A rival, for example, could seduce your love by singing your song to her."

"That's conceivable."

"That's ridiculous. Get off your backside, man, and do something before it's too late."

"There is nothing I can do. Besides, I have my responsibility."

"What responsibility?"

"I'm watching over my twelve white geese in the enclosure over there. I've been fattening them for Christmas and guarding them day and night. I know you would whip one as soon as my back was turned."

"Now that you mention it, I did have my eye on those geese. You've been stalling them extremely well. But I will take only one. You will hardly miss one from so many."

"I have twelve geese, for the twelve days of Christmas."

"Absolutely superfluous. Why take so much bother to provide yourself with excess? You would be better off forgoing a dinner. And if you were to let me have just one of your geese, you would have no more worry about me. You could concentrate on your song, make it so much better."

"All right then. I'll let you take just one, that thin one in the corner, provided you don't create a fluster and frighten the others."

"It was the plump one in the middle I had my eye on."

"Not that one. That is the pride of my flock, intended to grace my table on Christmas Day."

"But if I were to accept any other, there would always be the temptation to come back for the best. Then your mind could never be at ease. Whereas if you give me that plump goose now, you can get back to your song with an undivided mind."

"All right," said Thornton. "It makes sense. You may take the plump one, but don't go frightening the rest."

"Perhaps you should pass it out to me yourself. That way there will be least fuss."

Thornton closed the window and went out to the enclosure. He singled out the plump goose, and with a deft hand he gathered it into the crook of his arm. Smoothing down its feathers he removed it from the enclosure. He stretched it out to the fox.

"Thank you," said the fox. "And you might consider taking singing lessons." With a quick snap he took the goose and turned back to the hill.

Thornton stood watching the fox until he gradually merged into the russet of the hillside. Only the white speck of his goose was visible to the last.

When he returned to the house Thornton sat down again at his table inside the window. He tried to pick up the scattered notes of his song. But he could not concentrate. His mind was on the plump white goose he had surrendered so easily and on the eleven others that were still in his charge.

O'Dowd and
The Mermaid

On the strand near Scurmore stands a cluster of rocks called the Seven Children of the Mermaid, flowing over which the incoming tide generates a strange wailing noise. Legend explains that a mermaid, returning to sea, changed to stone the seven children she had begotten of a human husband.

WHEN O'DOWD DISCOVERED THAT HIS wife had gone, he felt as if a great weight had been lifted off his back. When he could not find his children, he panicked. Driven by an immediate impulse, he sprinted down to the seashore, to the place where he had first encountered her. The tide was out and still ebbing. He was able to pick his way along the base of the cliff, nimbly side-stepping the concentrations of green sea-lettuce, for fear he should slip and break his bones. Then there would be no chance of his saving the children. He passed the little rockpool out of which he had once picked the drowned body of little Caitlin, their first-born. He gave the pool a quick glance, but the children were all too big for that pool to be a hazard to them now.

He rounded the end of the cliff face and reached the secluded cove called Seals' Pool where he had first laid eyes on her. He thought she might have chosen to leave from the same place where she had come ashore. But there was no sign of her, and no sign of the children. He was momentarily relieved.

Seals' Pool had not changed in the slightest over the many

years since he had last visited it. The great cavern still yawned darkly at the far end of the cove. The flat rocks and the jagged rocks that he had known so intimately were still there, still covered with wrack and mussels.

His heart was full as he surveyed the rocky coastline from this vantage point. Here he had come in the old days to escape from the world, to be alone, to indulge in the delicious terror of total isolation. Those were the days after he had inherited his estate, when he spent more time examining the wild shores and rocky inlets that surrounded his estate on three sides than he did cultivating the rich fields in between.

There was no sign of his wife, or of his seven children. The children could not take to the water. Little Caitlin had proved that. They had enjoyed hours of diversion along the shore in their early days together, and used to bring Caitlin to play among the rocks. But, once, they forgot her for a few moments, and she strayed up to the little rockpool that was etched out at the base of the cliff. By the time they located her she had drowned, face downwards, reaching towards the straining fingers of the sea-anemones on the sandy bottom.

A cold shiver ran through O'Dowd's powerful frame. Where could they have gone? He hurried back to the house to check it once again, hoping they would all be there, hoping there would be a simple explanation of their temporary disappearance. But there was still no sign of anyone. He searched the rows of grey stables once more. There was no trace of them, neither a sign nor a sound, as if they had never existed.

He was not surprised by the departure of his wife; he had been more than half expecting it. They had always been strangers, even at the beginning, even during the elation of their first conjunction. However, at that time there were bonds, bonds of interest and curiosity, bonds of physical attraction. But such bonds unravel with time. And so it was. Finally, without ever articulating it, they found that they preferred each other in the absence than in the presence. All they had in common was their children, and now they were gone too.

It was on a summer's morning that he met her. He was dallying along the shore when he should have been labouring in the fields. Ambling along under the cliff face, he turned the corner to his favourite nook, Seals' Pool. He was arrested, astonished, by the sight of a girl, a girl of incredible beauty, swimming there in the cove in front of him. He stood transfixed, embarrassed. She was totally naked. He looked around to see where she had left her clothes, but couldn't see them anywhere, and, at first, he was puzzled by that. He marvelled at the locks of black hair clinging to her neck and to the white skin of her shoulders. He marvelled at the clean delicate line of her features, at the dreamy distant look in her eyes. She was swimming over and back and around the cove. She didn't spot O'Dowd for a long time, and he stayed lurking at the corner of the rock face, fascinated, excited.

Eventually she paused. It was then she cast her eye about and spotted O'Dowd skulking among the rocks. She fixed him with her gaze, quite unabashed by the situation. Slowly his awkwardness melted and he shuffled down to the edge of the pool. She cast out into the deep water again, diving, frolicking, smiling up at him. O'Dowd took this as an invitation, an invitation he could not possibly resist. He was a good swimmer. He peeled off his clothes and dived into the pool to join her.

She appeared delighted. Over and back they swam, splashing, diving under one another, laughing. It was O'Dowd's first experience of a woman, his first time to sport naked with a woman in the sun, first time to touch with pleasure the soft white flesh of a woman's breast, the first time to run his fingers, his lips, his tongue, along the firm white flesh of a woman's thigh. There was salt in her kisses, salt in every touch. She swam slowly now, almost floating, letting her arms and legs drift in the water languid as the brown oarweed underneath, langorous as the green fronds of dabberlocks tenderly flapping against her.

O'Dowd, inexperienced but with native instinct, took her, gently, there in the middle of the pool, to the helping heaving swell of the sea. Sated, they stretched out to rest and sun themselves on a flat rock that was covered with a quilt of bladder wrack, and when they took to making love again the squelching, and popping, and bursting of the bladder wrack made them laugh.

Evening came and the tide washed in over the rocks, the advancing waves began to lash the base of the cliff, and the little cove became submerged in the expanse of open sea. O'Dowd held her hand while he shifted his clothes further and further up the shore. She showed no inclination to go. It was as if she were now obliged to stay with him. O'Dowd was perplexed. Then, almost without thinking, he made a decision: he took up his clothes, pulled on his trousers and jacket, separating his long shirt. This he wrapped around her. She ran her arms through the sleeves, and he fastened the row of buttons. When she stood up the shirt fell mid-way on her thighs. O'Dowd was satisfied and led her by the hand over the pebbled beach and back through the fields to his house.

Convinced that they were nowhere on his headland estate, O'Dowd reluctantly decided that he would have to call on his neighbours and enquire whether they had seen his wife and seven children go past. His reluctance sprung from the lack of contact he had had with his neighbours over the years. She had always recoiled at the prospect of meeting anyone of his kind, and so he had allowed his friendships and kinships to slowly lapse. Eventually, they were living in almost total isolation, hostile to any encroachments from the outside world, like badgers in a set.

His neighbours were therefore surprised, almost alarmed, to see him. When he put his enquiry to them, they stared at him, uncomprehending, and exchanged bewildered glances among themselves. And when he turned his back to proceed with his quest, they shook their heads in resignation. "Poor O'Dowd has finally parted with the last of his wits," they agreed. "Wife! Seven children! He certainly concocted a good one when he was at it."

They were afraid he might come to harm so they pulled on their coats and bolted their doors to follow him, keeping their distance out of respect for his distressed state of mind.

Such was the way in which O'Dowd journeyed through the countryside, asking all he encountered whether they had seen a woman with seven children. All answered no, they had not, and were struck by the anguished tone of the question and the strange manner of the questioner. When they met the growing band of worried pursuers, they asked who the tormented stranger was, and were told that it was only O'Dowd, who lived alone on his small holding out on the point, and whose wits had evidently fled before the black dogs of loneliness.

O'Dowd followed the coast road, for he knew that she would never venture far from the sea, despite the ambivalence in her attitude to it that developed from the drowning of Caitlin. Afterwards she went to the shore only to gather winkles or carraigeen for the table, yet O'Dowd would find her gazing at the white tips of distant breakers when the brooding mood was upon her. However, she would not succumb to his enticements to go swimming in Seals' Pool, even when the coast was simmering in the heat of summer. And there were times when he tried his utmost to entice her down to Seals' Pool. They had failed afterwards to re-enact the magic of their first mating. In the warm bed on a winter's night, in the long grass of a meadow in high summer, it was always the same, mundane. Her cold flesh did not excite him the way it did in the sparkle of seaspray; and he sensed from her indifference that she too was losing her grip on that warm spur of pleasure. He found himself adopting the stratagem of closing his eyes, imagining her limbs entwined with green and brown shoots of sea-plants, her kisses savouring of brine; he found that she also was closing her eyes, and surmised that she too was trying to stimulate herself through similar wilful imaginings; it was as if not they but two other people were mating in another place at another time.

The frequent pregnancies provided a welcome relief from their cold mating rituals. The children came, one after the other, until there were seven of them surviving, growing up strong and healthy, and the rearing of these children filled O'Dowd's nights and days with contentment. But now they were gone.

The prospect of losing his children terrified O'Dowd. His consolation in life had been to watch them grow, to watch bone and muscle being hardened and tempered in that wild landscape, to watch eye and mind open with wonder to the world around them. He regretted not having been able to rear them according to the customs of his own people, not having had troops of kinsfolk around to mother them and father them and foster them, but yet he was satisfied that they were growing into full and forceful young men and women. Alienating the world had been the inevitable consequence of their union. She was what she was and nothing could change that.

O'Dowd too was the slave of his own nature. There were times when he was almost demented by the craving for human contact, for even a touch of warm human flesh. He began to fantasise about the women he saw going the road in the distance, imagined touching them, making love to them. There were times when he ran waist-high into the sea to try and quench the lust that was burning him mentally and physically.

Going along the sea road through Carrownabinna and Killeenduff, he had no thought of satisfying lust, no thought of the subtleties of child-rearing, only the gnawing anxiety that his children would come to harm, that he would never see them again.

On the bridge at Easkey, O'Dowd spotted a cluster of perennial loiterers, people who had spent their lives gazing down the roads or into the river, people who would have noticed any movement whatsoever in the area, a dandelion yielding its seeds to the wind or a trout snapping at a fly on the surface of the water. Yes, they had seen them: they had crossed the bridge earlier, full of purpose, a woman followed by seven children, and they had headed off along the coast. O'Dowd, greatly relieved, quickened his pace.

The band of pursuers slowed down when they saw O'Dowd pausing on the bridge. "The poor man is talking to himself," they whispered. "We had better decide what to do with him before he comes to harm."

They crammed into a public house beyond the bridge to refresh themselves and to decide on a course of action. "If he was intent on harming himself, he would have tried it long ago," some of them said, hoping for agreement to turn around and go home.

"He's in a strange mood all the same. It would be unneighbourly of us to surrender him to the whims of the world and he not totally in command of his senses." And this argument held sway.

In the meantime O'Dowd was following the shoreline with greater confidence, but he still did not catch as much as a glimpse of his wife and children in the distance. Dusk was setting in and he feared he would have to abandon his search to the darkness. Beyond Rathlee he was passing the derelict cottage known as the house of the Scarlet Widow when he noticed a young woman standing in the doorway looking out at him. He went over to make his enquiries.

She was sympathetic, said she knew what it was to lose her children, had watched the earthworm creep across her son's face and the rat make its nest in the hollow of his skull, had felt the cinders and the ashes of her embraced daughter sift into her own and fall together on the floor of their cottage. She would make a deal, take miles off his journey, and help him catch his wife before the darkness fell; he would have to return the favour, rifle the tomb of Canon Murphy in the nearby churchyard, gather his dust, and carry it with him; all he had to do was cast a fistful in the air every time he was unsure and she would be behind to blow the dust in the direction he should take; in that way she would have her ambition fulfilled, to see the dust of that reverend gentleman scattered for pigs to eat and dogs to shit on. For he it was who put a torch to her house, when she had rejected his continuous propositions, having barred the door against escape for herself and her two young children. He it was who put the rumour abroad that she had been a source of sin, that it was the hand of God that visited her house with fire; he who had dubbed her the Scarlet Widow.

O'Dowd would have bartered for her help even without the incentive of a righteous cause. She was as good as her word and each time he cast a fistful of dust into the air he saw it carried unambiguously on the wind. He was tempted several times to look behind and see if the tall beauty was following him, but she had asked him not to, and he resisted the temptation.

When he cast up his last handful of dust it lifted into the dark sky and streaked off emphatically in the direction of the long beach at Enniscrone. O'Dowd then turned around, but there was no one and nothing there. He hastened down to the beach, where the great white breakers rolled up the sandy incline. He was able to run without difficulty on the hard wet sand. About a mile down the beach he spotted her, and he spotted the children, all seven of them, in a cluster behind her. They were silhouetted against the faint glow of the western horizon. She was marching inexorably into the rolling tide. He ran and ran until his lungs were gasping and aching inside him.

Coming closer, he saw that she had waded out into the surf well ahead of the cluster of children, and he ran out into the water to get between them. The first wave that hit him almost knocked him over, but he found his feet and advanced slowly towards her. Her clothes were drenched and clung to her body in the intermissions between waves. She was glancing behind, conscious of his presence. Her face was impassive, betraying no sign of fear, or elation, or anger, or regret. On and on she went, and O'Dowd followed.

But when the crests of the breakers began to pass over his head, he took fright, realising that he was being lured to his death. He remembered, in consternation, the children and turned to fight his way back. The tide was flowing and carried him easily to the cluster of black shapes behind him. He could not make out which of them was which because their faces were lost in shadow. When he reached the first dark figure he wrapped his arms around his neck and dug his feet into the earth to hold the advance of all seven.

As if indignant at his intervention, the sea lashed him and dragged him and tried to break his grip, but O'Dowd held on with fierce determination releasing a scream from the bottom of his soul, a scream so intense that it silenced the thunder of the sea, a scream in whose modulations could be determined the anguish of birth and separation, the anguish of fear and apprehension for one's children, the anguish of despair.

His pursuing neighbours heard that scream and it filled them with dread. They were rushing up the strand, having discerned him in the distance advance into the sea. But when they reached the spot they were driven back by the heavily flowing tide. Despite their searching of the shore they could find no trace of O'Dowd and were forced eventually towards the single bleak conclusion.

Sheltering in the sand dunes, they kept vigil until dawn. By then the sea had begun to ebb. Their eyes were fixed on the spot where O'Dowd had disappeared. Out of the receding water in that exact position they saw a cluster of rocks rising from the foam. By the time the water was knee-high these rocks were standing clear and upright and unusual against the sweep of sandy beach.

They waded out into the water to inspect them, and, to their amazement, there they found O'Dowd, his lifeless body wrapped around the foremost of these rocks. They tried to release him, but, drowned and stiff as he was, he clenched the rock with an unnatural grasp. No limpet could have clung more tightly. They located a wooden stake among the sand dunes and used this to lever his arms free of the rock. They used their belts to strap his arms to his body and to hold his feet together. Then, lifting him, they shouldered his considerable weight, and began the journey home.

BIRDS

What drove Sweeney mad?
What drove him
to forsake his cosy cottage?
What drove the poor man
to roost in trees
                and sing
                            and chirp
as if he were a finch or a robin?
No
    it wasn't the court order
    nor the bailiff's car
    circling the farm
No
    it wasn't the collapse
    of the dairy market
    nor the imported New Zealand butter
No
    it wasn't the lonely nights
    and the bad television programmes.

It was the birds.

Sweeney
        was an old-style farmer
        rose at noon
               and not a moment before
        kept a pair of short-horn cows
            four or five heifers
            a donkey
            and a flock of squawking hens
        planted a rood of spuds
        harvested

            two hundredweight of oats
            from the sheltered garden
            behind the house
            a row of cabbages
            for himself
            a row of mangolds
            for the poor old donkey.
That was the full extent
of this man's husbandry.

But Sweeney's pride and joy
was his sixteen-acre field.
Rotund
         like the great curve
         of the earth itself
it raised its soft breast
                        above
the ragged shapes
              of walls and hedges
              drains and boulders
              that defined the limits
              of adjoining paltry plots.

Never
      did a plough's edge
      disturb the green turf
      in the sixteen-acre field.
Never
      did Sweeney
      force a rank unnatural growth
      by spreading the powdered wonder
      from the plastic bags.
And yet
        his sweet and buxom field
        nourished his cattle
        from autumn until spring.
And when he harvested
                     the lush meadows
                     of the summer

that crop of hay could fodder
the entire livestock
                of the whole townland.

Sweeney's delight
                to lie in the long meadows
                of his sixteen-acre field
                when the high sun
                of June
                gave true licence
                for laziness.
Sweeney's delight
                to watch the skylarks
                dive and soar
                soar and dive
                high
                above the waving grasses
                of his sixteen-acre field.
Sweeney's delight
                to listen
                to the meadow birds
                the cuckoo in the morning
                the corncrake at night
                raising a continual chorus
                from the five corners
                of his sixteen-acre field.

But
    summers passed
and Sweeney
            was advancing
                      in years
           never married
           never fathered a child
and yet it seemed
that every added year
choirs
      of cuckoos

        skylarks and corncrakes
serenaded his middle age.

Sweeney
        came to love
                these vagrant singers who came
                to nestle
                in the soft bosom
                of his sixteen-acre field
        never mowed the meadow
        until after Garland Sunday
        when every chick was fledged
        and every migrant spirit
        had taken to the air
                again.

People marvelled
at the chorus of birdsong
rising
        from Sweeney's field.
Travellers came
            from distant far-flung places
            to listen.
Hadn't heard a cuckoo
in years
        they said.
The last corncrake
had long been silenced
in the flat plains
that they inhabited
            they said.

Sweeney
        conscious of privilege
        waited longer
        for the fledgling corncrakes
        to vacate his meadow
        before he cut his hay.

From under Gogol's Nose

But August
\qquad never smiled
\qquad on his benevolence
\qquad sent rain year after year
his crop
\qquad lay sodden
\qquad turned mouldy grey
\qquad rotted on the ground
before he could gather it
into the shelter of his haggard.

Turn to silage
\qquad said the Man
\qquad from the Department.
A good field like that
you'd get two cuttings
\qquad\qquad easily
one in June
another late July
feed twenty head of cattle
from November
\qquad through to March
what's wrong with you
everyone is at it
then you might be able
to pay your lawful rates.

Turn to silage
\qquad said the horn-rimmed
\qquad Bank Manager.
Much more profitable
improve
modernise
keep up with the times
or go to the wall
simple really
moral dilemmas are bad for business
and then there's the problem of your mortgage.

Birds

Turn to silage
            said the Parish Priest.
No money
in hay or sentimentality.
Render to Caesar
            the coins
but keep the five-pound-notes
                    for God.
What about the dues, man,
What about the dues?

One more summer
            thought Sweeney
one good year
and all will be well.

Amazing
said the man with the field-glasses
            every last corncrake is there
            not another left
                    in the whole country
            totally extinct
            not a meadow left
            to nest in.
            And listen
            to those cuckoos
said the man with the zoom lens
            not many of them left
                    either.

            What about the skylarks
said the man with the notebook
            doesn't it sound
            as if every last one
            has found asylum
            in the long grass
                    of that meadow?

From under Gogol's Nose

      Yes, it's amazing!
      Truly wonderful!
      It's a miracle surely!

When the three of them
had driven off
         down the road
in the big Mercedes car
Sweeney trudged home
            to his cold cottage
            and his empty cupboards.

Silage
      said the Man from the Department
      waving his rate-demands.
Silage
      said the Bank Manager
      producing a court-order.
Silage
      said the Parish Priest
      opening a greasy collection book.

Another wet August
and Sweeney was utterly ruined.
Another hard winter
brought Sweeney to his knees.
The cows were gone
and the heifers
even the hens
all but the donkey
      that nobody wanted.
Dry spuds with salt
crushed oats that made black porridge
whatever meat the dole-money bought
dull fare
      for any man's table
worse
      for a lone bachelor's.

The next time
            the high sun
            drew the green blades
Sweeney resolved
            to put an end to poverty
            to slice the long stems
                        and harvest them
            to sell the crop
            and raise himself
                        upright
                        in his farmer's wellingtons
            to pay
                        the government
                                    their rates
                        the bank
                                    their mortgage
                        and the Parish Priest
                                    his dues.

Late June
            as was the custom
            among progressive farmers
Sweeney hired
            a Ferguson silage-maker
            powerful engine
            and a vicious set of cutting teeth.

At dawn
      Sweeney
                  drove the great tractor
                  into the field.
The Parish Priest
the Bank Manager
and the Department Inspector
                        arrived
                        and perched on the gate
                        to watch.

From under Gogol's Nose

Never
        had the rasping chorus of the corncrake
        seemed so loud.
Never had the deep-throated cuckoo
       overflowed
        with such spontaneous force
as if the whole meadow
     the entire sixteen-acre field
had been transformed
into one great orchestra
of vibrating stems
the rising melody
             blending
                    in mid-air
with the falling contra-puntal sweetness
of the skylark.

Only the three grey crows
on the iron gate
         were silent.

Sweeney
      stamped on the pedal
      revved
           the loud motor
until he could hear
nothing
       but the screeching monotone
       of pistons
       and the prolonged
       fart of the exhaust
then drove at the field
        straight across the centre
        straight to the heart
Then round the field
          and round
pedal to the floor
steering wheel

Birds

             fiercely gripped
cuckoos taking flight
long-legged corncrakes
                chasing distractedly
mangled chicks and eggs
mown down
        dismembered
sucked clean up
and blown
        in reeling atoms
        through the steel shafts
        of the silage cutter
into the pulped carnage in the trailer.

The three crows
            motionless
            looked on
with the cold eye
of the predator
waiting to inherit the earth.

The field
        shorn
        bare as a crag
Sweeney released the pedal
        braked and halted
        stepped down from the cab.
Everywhere
           the traces of plundered nests
           smear of gashed eggs
           blood and feathers
           sliced limbs
                scattered everywhere.
No escape.
Even the cuckoo's
chameleon deception
              mocked
              by mechanical slaughter.

From under Gogol's Nose

And the silence
    the terrifying nothingness
in the vast hemisphere
        of the heavens.

Silence broken
        by the ugly raucous delight
        of the three grey crows
        perched on the gate.

Sweeney listened.
Not even the faintest echo
    of cuckoo or corncrake
not a trace
    of air-blown warbling
from a distant skylark
nothing
    but the turgid silence
    and the vulgar noise of the crows applauding the
    applauding the wisdom of his deed.

Sweeney looked towards the gate.
Well done
    said the Department Inspector
that's a fine crop.
It will fetch
a fair shilling
    added the Bank Manager.
And God will be pleased
don't forget the talents
    said the Parish Priest
and don't forget me
when you reap your reward
caw
    caw
        caw.

Sweeney

                        leaped into the driver's seat
                        once more
                        turned the ignition
                        revved the engine
and
        with smoke steaming behind him
drove the tractor
                        with impetuous motion
                        straight
                        at the iron gate.
The crows fluttered their wings
in surprise and fright
rose awkwardly
                        off the gate
and scattered
uttering coarse obscenities
as
    the tractor struck
    made bits of their perch
    crossed the road
    to lodge its impact
    in the soft bank
                        beyond.

Sweeney descended from the tractor
            and returned
            to his sixteen-acre field.
No sound at all now
all silent like the stars
            like the grave.
Sweeney fell on his knees
weeping
            and kneeling there
            among the littered remains
            of the last colony
            of meadow birds
he began to imitate their sounds
crake-crake

Birds

    crake-crake
       crake-crake
cuck-oo
  cuck-coo
     cuck-coo
twitter twitter twitter .
He arose
   and began to run about the field
    flapping his arms
    and calling
as loud as he was able
twitter twitter
    cuck-coo
      crake-crake crake-crake.

The policeman
    who came
     to clear the blocked road
radioed an ambulance
   and a squad of keepers
    from the mental hospital.
As soon as they arrived
they pursued the chirping Sweeney
but he
   eluded them
   and fled across the countryside.
The flight
   was wild
   abandoned
the pursuit relentless
   tough
but
  as night fell
Sweeney reached Alternan
and escaped into the trees
     of Farnan's sacred wood.